SURFACE TENSION is a unique collection of six dark tales, which delve deep into the undercurrents of human psychology. Ghosts, heavenly creatures and magic beings find fantastical ways to deliver messages of warning or redemption. From a widow longing to be reunited with her husband, to a mother trapped by guilt, these stories reveal how life's tragic events can change our perception and lead to unexpected consequences. The results are delightful stories that charm, intrigue and scare in equal measure.

Works by the same author

HALF LIFE

URBAN CREATURES

Also available as audio-book: essentialaudiobooks.com

❋ Surface Tension

Sarah Gray

Claret Press

CLARET PRESS

Copyright © 2016 Sarah Gray
The moral right of the author has been asserted.

Cover design by Ginny Wood
Cover and story illustrations © 2015 Alodie Fielding
www.thecrookedstyle.com

ISBN paperback: 978-1-910461-11-2

ISBN ebook: 978-1-910461-12-9

A CIP catalogue record for this book is available from the
British Library.

This paperback or the ebook can be ordered from all
bookstores and from Claret Press, as well as eplatforms
such as Amazon and ibooks.

claretpress.com

For my brothers & sisters

Acknowledgments

Massive thanks to Katie Isbester for loving the stories in the first place, and for all her hard work and acute editing skills in making them the best they can be. To Laura Emsden for her thoughtful and precise feedback and Meg Wilson for her keen eyes. Thanks also to Alodie Fielding for her beautiful artwork, which completes the storytelling. Gratitude goes to my family, friends and those others who have provided enough juicy material to write endless stories. You won't know who you are, but you're in there, somewhere. Thank you for the inspiration.

Contents

Switch

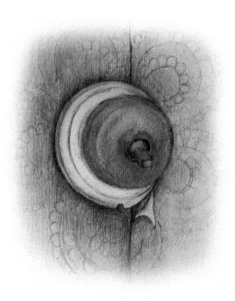

She'd never seen that light switch before. Straining her eyes across the dark bedroom, she could just make out its shape. Small and round, it protruded to a blunt point. It must be a trick of the light. Similar to those grotesque faces that had emerged from the flowers smothering her childhood's bedroom

9

curtains. Her parents' verdict: an overactive imagination. Coral had been denied her repeated plea to exchange the 'perfectly good' curtains for something less frightening.

When she grew up, the faces in the curtains disappeared. Despite how stupid it was, she still carried a secret fear of the unknown, a fear of the threats that nestle amongst ordinary things.

Slipping her hand from beneath the covers, she flicked on her bedside lamp. The bright light hurt her eyes. Shutting her lids tight, she kept them closed until the pain subsided. On blinking them open, the section of vivid purple wall where the switch had been was clear and flat. Her overactive imagination again.

Three days later the switch appeared again.

This time it was in the living room. She was knitting a jumper for her son. Frustrated at dropping a stitch, she looked away to rest her eyes and there it was, the same small, neat mound. This time she couldn't blame a night-time hallucination. Placing her knitting to one side, she stood up, staring at the unwelcome switch. She wondered if it would turn on her lights. The idea was silly; of course it couldn't be connected to anything. Unless it was a new addition that her son had ordered the electricians to install without her knowledge, adding another period feature to her recently renovated living room. After the fire, her son had insisted they restore the room to the original Victorian. Opening up the fireplace and choosing vintage items had made it 'just so'. At first she'd resisted. Keeping it as her husband had wanted made him feel close, warding off the suddenness of his death.

Richard had had the house modernised just after they'd met, and he'd been so excited about the surprise she hadn't known about it until it was completed. He was fond of contemporary styles and wanted her to have 'all the mod cons' for their life together. Brash, bold colours stylish in the 1970s were used, and each room had a different theme. He'd installed gas central heating, a fitted kitchen and a bathroom suite. As soon as she had seen the house from the street, she'd loved it. It resembled the type she drew as a child: detached, symmetrical and neat; her idea of the perfect home. A shiny black door in the centre offered entry to its four floors. She laughed aloud with shock when she saw the rainbow interior; it was not to her taste at all. She thought it ugly and was disappointed to live in a beautiful old house that had been turned into a night club.

She had dreamed about them choosing the décor together, making their first decisions as a married couple. Never mind. Richard had already done it all for her and she wanted to please him, so she never told him. When married life became routine, Richard spent most of his time at home in his office on the top floor, and she in the lounge, which backed onto the enormous garden. She loved having a generous garden full of over-hanging trees and burgeoning plants. Watching the birds that came and went throughout the year made her happy and she felt gratified she could offer them a home.

But the switch was neither from the original 1880s fittings nor from the 1970s.

"It must be Bakelite, 1940s I'd guess." Coral listened to her son's reply.

"And you're sure you didn't ask for it. No, no why would you. Okay sweetpea, I know. Come and try on your new jumper soon. Yes, yes okay, love you too."

Coral wavered, still holding the turquoise telephone receiver in her hand. He obviously thought she was going batty. Maybe she was. Maybe she'd ordered the electricians to install it and had then forgotten. Although he didn't say, James blamed her for the fire. She'd only left the candle for a moment, but it was enough. Her armchair was destroyed, as was everything within a few feet of it, and the ceiling and walls were black with smoke damage. No need to dwell on damage already done. The switch would probably be gone when she got back to the living room and she could forget all about it.

It was still there.

She checked the builders' invoices for any listing of the light switch. Nothing. Coral began to panic. She couldn't remember anything about it at all. James was right, she was losing her mind. Confusion slowly gave way to curiosity. She could flick it. What was the worst that could happen, and surely it wouldn't work anyway. Walking slowly towards it she held out her hand, but stopped just a few inches from the nipple. She was afraid. And excited.

"Come on Coral, you're not a baby. Do it." She looked around the room waiting for someone to tell her off. Silence reigned.

It clicked with crisp perfection.

Before she saw anything she heard a loud scraping noise, as if metal was being dragged across concrete. Her excitement faded. Holding her fingertips on the switch, she turned her head slightly towards the noise. Her eyes followed.

At the fireplace was a faint shadow. Initially it was difficult to make out its shape, but as she stared detail became clearer. A figure knelt, with a scarf tied around its delicate head. Coral assumed it was a teenage girl. She was bending forward on her knees, engulfed by the large fireplace. With both fists she clasped a hand shovel, huge in her slender fingers. In a repeated motion, she scraped the tool from the back of the fireplace to the front. Coral couldn't see any detail around the girl, just her transparent figure. The rhythm of the scraping increased, speeding up, the sound getting louder and louder, drilling into her head. She wanted to scream for the girl to stop but heard the door open and saw the girl twist her head around towards it. Her expression was one of genuine fear. The girl's quiet terror engulfed Coral. Fear arrested her body, stealing her power and leaving her limbs loose and useless. Following the girl's gaze, Coral could see nothing, but the girl's eyes were those of a trapped animal anticipating cruelty. Unable to watch any longer, Coral flicked the switch and the girl disappeared.

After three weeks Coral still found it difficult to get the girl's expression out of her mind. Lying awake at night, she stared into the dark space in front of her. The house changed, now that it had a secret. She felt an uneasy blend of fear and curiosity. Even though Richard had died in the house, it had been their home and she'd never considered leaving it. He'd fallen down the stairs and broken his neck. Living with the nearness of death made even the sight of fresh-cut flowers remind her of the fragile nature of life. She couldn't have them in the house; watching them decay and die unsettled her. That its past occupants could be troubled had never occurred to her. History forced itself into her present and she needed to know who were these people invading her home. They might want to hurt her or force her out.

But if the girl had died in the house that might be the reason Coral could see her. If so, maybe it was possible to see Richard. He could still be with her. A frisson of joy, absent since his death, flowed around her system. Instead of dreading the switch, she longed for its reappearance.

*****

Forcing the shovel into the hard ground she struggled to lift the soil out, but it kept tumbling back in. Scraping it out over and again, she found that the hole never got any deeper, and she grew wearier with each repetition. Her weariness became edged with panic as she realised to save herself she had to dig deep and would only fail.

Dawn was breaking into her bedroom as the nightmare jolted her from sleep, her heart beating fast with fear. She stumbled onto the landing, felt for the light and flicked it. For a few moments of blurred confusion, she didn't realise she'd turned the Bakelite switch on. Noise surrounded her, dull and consistent. Terrified she grabbed for the switch, but the regular one had replaced it. The noise continued.

Pushing the heavy living room door open, she stood in the entrance looking for the switch. It wasn't there. The noise was no nearer, but it sounded as if someone was trying to escape from a locked room. A desperate banging on a door and pulling on its handle, rattling back and forth, *bang, bang, bang*. She could smell smoke. The repetitive hammering felt as if it were hitting her skull, confusing her more, terrifying her with its relentlessness.

Stumbling around the house, she searched each room for the switch, the noise telling her someone was trapped and couldn't escape. Coral's throat constricted in frustration at the absent switch and her failure to find the source of the noise. Panic overwhelmed her. She grabbed at a door, but it was locked, she pulled at its handle and banged on the wood.

Smoke slithered under the threshold. Coral cried out with anger, covering her ears and screwing her eyes together tight, trying to block it out. As she closed herself to the noise, it stopped and silence penetrated her house. The door crept open.

Exhausted, Coral slumped against the wall, her breathing slowing its pace, her heart returning to something reasonable. It made no sense to her. She couldn't understand the noise and what it meant, but the feeling of being trapped saturated her.

*****

Finally. She'd managed to get James to come and try on his jumper. After her husband died, she'd taken up knitting professionally. At first it had just been something to do but it soon developed into a business, specialising in recreating vintage knits. It didn't make her a huge income, but she was good at it and proud of her work. Whenever she was working on a new style or pattern she used her son as a model. He endured it with good grace, but she rarely saw him wearing one of her jumpers.

Coral pulled a batch of cheese scones from the oven and placed them on the work surface. Her kitchen was spotless. She didn't mind mess in any other room, but the kitchen needed to be ordered and scrubbed clean. The turquoise walls were topped with brown and turquoise floral tiles, which met with the work surfaces midway down the wall. The smell of baking lingered as she loaded the scones and cake onto the tray. Picking it up, she turned and started to walk towards the door. The switch rested behind the entrance to the hallway. China clinked as she jumped, and a single cup fell, smashing as it hit the ground. Coral didn't want to see the girl in pain again, but this could also be Richard. She flicked the switch.

Standing at a deep, white sink the girl was drying a china oven dish. It looked heavy, but she handled it well, her small hand rubbing the surface with ease. This time the scene was clearer, still opaque but the detail was easier to make out and things appeared more solid. With her back to the door, the girl was humming a jolly tune. A heavy door slammed making the girl jump and the dish slipped to the floor, smashing to pieces. A tall man stepped forward and slapped the girl to the ground. Coral, sickened by the force of the impact, flicked the switch and the scene disappeared. She hadn't seen the man's face but he was neat, slender and upright.

Coral knew what she'd seen was real. She was terrified, but she must find a way to help the girl. If there were ghosts trapped in their cycle of life then maybe she could try and put them to rest, possibly have the house exorcised. She'd never been religious; her parents had considered anything supernatural as ridiculous 'mumbo-jumbo', including the idea of God. There was little else she could do, maybe she could talk to the girl, try to disturb the cycle somehow. Richard would solve the problem. She just had to work out how to contact him.

Coral had calmed down by the time James arrived. As she watched him enter the living room she was surprised by how much he'd grown to look like his father. He was tall and slim with a floppy fringe fashionable when he was in his late teens and a fan of Britpop. It was now streaked with grey. In character though, James was much more relaxed and playful, almost the opposite of Richard.

"Hello Mum." Raising a hand almost in a salute, he crossed the living room and gave her a peck on the cheek. He slumped in the wingback chair opposite Coral and began to pour the tea. It wasn't until he had finished filling the two cups that he looked at his mother's face.

He frowned, scrutinising her. "You look tired."

"Do I?" She laughed and brought her hand to her forehead. "Maybe a bit."

James handed her a floral teacup, which matched the turquoise and brown kitchen colour combination.

"Sup on this. You'll be revived." He laughed. "So where's this mysterious switch then?" He looked around the room.

"Oh, it was nothing."

"Nothing? Mum, are you okay?" She stirred her tea, not looking directly at her son. He smiled, knowing her dislike of being challenged. If pushed, she would change the subject and ignore the question.

"It's looking good in here now. And the smell of paint has almost gone. See, I was right about having it restored. You should do the kitchen next."

"James, don't go on. I don't want to and it doesn't need it." She frowned, a fake grimace.

"Think how much more it would be worth if it was fully restored to its original glory." He flicked an elegant hand to indicate the house.

"I don't care about the money, and anyway, who knows what secrets might come out."

"Mum, really? You've lived here for years. I'm sure there's nothing you don't know about this house."

"But I don't know anything, not really. Only when it was built and that your Dad left it to me when he died. I wondered if you'd found anything out when you were doing the living room?"

"You're becoming curious in your old age. Didn't realise I was looking for secrets. Why?"

"Nothing, but I suppose all old houses must have a past."

"But this has always been such a friendly house. Except for, well, you know, and I wasn't scared of Dad."

"Why would you be?" Coral stopped for a moment in astonishment and then continued. "Do you ever think he could still be here? Only we can't see him?"

"What do you mean? No, of course not. Mum, if you're feeling tired, why don't you go on holiday? Laura and I would be happy to pay. Please don't complain. We want to."

"No." Coral shook her head. "Thank you, but I can't go away, not now."

"Well, the offer stands. If knitting and the Old Dears' Book Club are more important than your health then that's up to you." They both laughed.

James hadn't stayed long. Coral sat in the living room trying to knit, listening for any change in the natural sounds of the house. Shadows seemed to reflect across the walls. Scenes played out with faint outlines and figures lingered, but all these lived in the corner of

Coral's eye. Living out its history, the house was in constant motion, the past greedy, pushing for its place in the present. Despite the violence to the girl that Coral had witnessed, there had been something serene and content about her when she'd been working. Coral took comfort from that. She was also frightened for her, continuing her chores under the threat of cruelty, locked in a cycle of domestic drudgery and fear. Maybe the girl had been locked up, and the feelings of dread and terror she'd felt were hers. Having only ever known a loving family, Coral couldn't understand the need for someone to inflict terror onto another person. Unnecessary pain baffled her. She had been a nervous child who sought safety, and her parents, with stoic cheer, had helped her overcome some of her worries.

Like her parents, Richard had dealt with everything. She had liked the way he'd taken control of their lives. It made her feel loved and cared for. When he'd died she'd had to look after the housekeeping. Although he'd left her well provided for, learning to cope had been a struggle. Raw grief had overwhelmed her, and she hadn't ever been quite present, using only enough of her brain to complete mechanical tasks, hardly aware of what she was doing and not remembering it once it was done. After time, she slid into a comfortable routine. The switch had changed that. Coral felt as if her brain had been flicked on.

*****

The internet was never her first solution to problem solving. 'In her day' the internet didn't exist, and she'd never needed answers before. With her two middle fingers she tapped out the address. Various locations with the same address popped up in the search. She added the postcode. A link appeared: *After the fire, 1969.* She clicked on it. The blog was called 'Local History Now' and focused on local architectural restoration. There were four photographs. The first had her husband's family at the centre. They were lined up in front of a magnolia bush, which Coral recognised as the one at the bottom of her garden. The caption read: *Mr Ronald Blake, with his children Richard and Cordelia, 1958.*

Being a little younger than Coral, Cordelia must have been around five years old, but Coral couldn't make out any facial detail as the figures were small and blurred. She was willowy, as was Richard, and his wiry figure made her smile. She wished she had known him as a young man.

Below were three photographs of the house. One had been taken when it was newly built in 1880, and one was from 1970 just before she and Richard married. But it was the middle one that attracted Coral's attention. It showed the house burnt out, almost destroyed, its charred skeleton exposed. Underneath it read: *Ronald Blake unfortunately lost his life, and his son, Richard Blake, restored the house within a year.* Coral was shocked. Richard had never told her the house had burnt down, or that his father had been killed in the fire. That explained the complete refit. Richard had obviously decided to restore the house's exterior to its original state, but redesigned the interior. He'd told her it was for her.

She found the email address for the man who wrote the blog and sent him a message to ask if he had any more information about the house, or about the Blake family. He billed himself as a local historian, so he would know more than her about the past, even her own husband's past. They had been so happy, but she knew so little about him.

They'd met at work. He was the managing director of a local firm, and she had joined the company just after qualifying from secretarial college. Coral had done well considering her background: most of her school friends had left school at fifteen to work in the local factory. She had worked hard because she wanted to help take some financial burden off her parents, not because she'd wanted a career. However, she enjoyed working in an office where she was expected to be well dressed and efficient. Her relationship with Richard had been straightforward from the beginning. They worked well together and he appreciated her compliant nature. It was only a few months before he asked her to marry him. Her parents were shocked that someone of his stature was prepared to marry an office girl, but made it clear that Coral shouldn't 'look a gift horse in the mouth'. Coral admitted she'd never actually asked him that much about his past; she lived in the present and was content to do so. They'd had complete trust and it wouldn't have occurred to her that anything was different from her own understanding.

It took four days for the historian, Mr Marchant, to reply.

RE: ENQUIRY

Dear Mrs Blake,

Delighted to hear from you.

I knew your husband before you and he met. He came to me after the fire to give him advice on how to restore the house exterior. It's a shame he didn't introduce us.

I was very pleased that he spent a lot of time and money getting the restoration right. I can't say I was very impressed with his choice for the interior, however, but each to his own.

The house had been in your husband's family since it was built in 1880. The fire was, of course, a family tragedy, and the inheritance had been settled only a short time before you two married. I'm surprised he never discussed it with you. I've included a copy of the local newspaper article reporting the fire.

I hope this information is useful to you. If you'd like me to look further into the Blake family I'd be happy to do so. A donation to support my work – I'm currently collecting to help restore St George's – would be most welcome.

Thank you.

Yours sincerely,

M. Marchant.

Local Architectural Historian

According to the article, no one really understood why the fire had started, which raised suspicions of arson. The article implied that Richard's father had committed suicide, depressed by the death of his daughter. Coral was stunned. This had happened not long before she had met Richard and he'd kept this all to himself.

Richard had been intensely reserved and rarely spoke of his childhood or family. He communicated with his eyebrows: lowering them in a frown of disagreement or raising one in a sardonic question. Being sixteen years older than her, she assumed it was because he was of a different generation. When he mentioned his past, he'd often start with 'Where

I grew up', as if it had been some place other than here. As Coral knew his family had been well off, she imagined he had lived in a large house in the country. It never occurred to her that he might have grown up in this very house. He had told her he'd had a sister about her age, but she had died. His father returned from abroad for the funeral but found it hard to continue with his life, his grief a terrible burden. As a result, he'd become a recluse and then died. Richard didn't say how Cordelia had died, and Coral was happy not to dwell on it. Who wanted to talk about death anyway, and it must have been horrible for all of them. Coral had once suggested that if they had a girl, they could name the baby after his sister. He'd just stared at her with such a steady baleful gaze so she never mentioned it again. Besides, they never had another child. After James's birth, their relationship developed into a close friendship, passion no longer a priority.

Coral switched off the computer. She decided to ring James and talk to him about it. He'd know what to do. At the bottom of the stairs, above the telephone, sat the switch. She stared at it, scared at what the house might reveal to her this time. But she longed to see Richard. Coral flicked it. The sound of a loud and repeated thumping noise, as if someone was falling down the stairs, surrounded her. She recognised it. Memories of Richard tumbling to the bottom of the stairs played out in her head, the panic for the telephone, and James's screams.

She smiled and said out loud, "It's him." She would be able to ask him everything now and make up for her previous lack of curiosity. She wouldn't tell James anything. He'd only tell her it was her imagination.

After that, Coral wouldn't leave the house. She was sure Richard was there with her. A constant excitement churned in her stomach, as if she were a child on Christmas Eve. He would contact her directly at some point, she was sure of it, so she just had to keep waiting. But the wait was becoming too long. It had been weeks since she had last seen the switch, and she'd heard nothing from Mr Marchant. He was first to break the silence.

RE: ENQUIRY

Dear Mrs Blake,

I'm so sorry it's been this long. My work has been overwhelming, please do forgive me.

Thank you for your pending donation to the restoration fund. I assure you that every penny we raise will be used efficiently and wholly for this excellent cause. It's only due to the generosity of people such as yourself that we are able to perform this important work.

I've completed an initial check of the entire census up

until 1911 and in terms of the family at that time Richard's great-grandfather, Angus (54), and his grandparents, James (26) and Dorothy (24), were living in the house. There was also a maid, Elizabeth Castle (19), and a cook, Margaret Salmon (38), also registered as living in the house.

Apologies for my brevity, but I will keep searching other sources and let you know any more details as I find them.

No rest for the wicked, fundraising is such hard work.

Yours,

M. Marchant.

Local Architectural Historian

It was possible, then, that the girl she had seen was Elizabeth, the young servant of Richard's grandparents. There was no mention of who the man could be. It seemed impossible that anyone from Richard's family could be so cruel. The next time she saw the girl she'd look for clues and details of the period of the house, clothes or furniture.

Late one evening she climbed the narrow staircase to Richard's attic study. Coral had hesitated at the bottom, afraid to go up. The attic had been

29

the servant quarters when the house had first been built. It was so quiet and cut off from the rest of the house that it was the only place Richard felt he was able to concentrate. She wasn't welcome up there. No one was. So she never went, not even after his death. But if she were to help the girl she must try and find as much information as possible. What she would find, if anything, she wasn't sure. To make it clear that she wasn't barging in like a barbarian, she gently knocked and waited a moment or two before pushing open the door. "I'm sorry, Richard," she whispered as she entered the room.

Unused to entering his sanctuary, it felt as if it belonged to an unknown house. Coral traced her hand over his desk; her fingers left long streaks along the surface as they disturbed the dust. The ceiling was low and cobwebs hung from the deep green walls, creating soft edges, enveloping her. She opened a desk drawer and peered in. Scared of discovery, she looked over her shoulder, waiting for Richard to walk in and find her looking through his private things. She lifted each item out, but they were mundane everyday objects. Coral replaced them and repeated the ritual for all four drawers. Nothing of any use was in any of them. She spun on the chair, and as it came to a halt, she was facing the switch.

The girl was sweeping the floor and humming her tune. She moved in a square that only covered half of the room, which must have been where the original rooms would have been divided, but she stopped in front of a picture and straightened it, then looked back towards Coral as if staring right at her. She then bent down and swept the dust into her metal pan and walked out of the door.

Coral followed. When she turned the corner onto the tiny landing the girl was gone. Only the echo of the tune remained. Coral returned to the study. The switch had disappeared. Coral looked around the room, desperate to find something that might help her. The picture the girl had straightened was once again crooked. Coral approached it and took it down from its hook. Underneath was a small safe. Coral had had no idea it was there. There must be something important in it and she had to find someone to get it open.

Her mind churned with possibilities, crowded with ideas about why the girl lingered, how she was connected with her family, and how Coral might save her. Not only Richard but also his father had died in her house, but there were still no clues as to who The Slender Man could be. It was possible he had died in her house too. Coral tried not to sleep. To miss the small window when the switch appeared would be unbearable. Instead, she jolted awake, still sitting in her armchair, her knitting having fallen to the floor in a tangled mess. Her nightmares were a confused narrative of the girl's suffering and her husband falling down the stairs. These two traumas linked together in a looped cycle played over and again – Richard and the girl both falling, indistinguishable from one another. Too exhausted to eat properly, she forced herself to heat soup but left it, the half empty bowl cold at her side.

Coral needed to make some sense out of everything she'd learned so far. It wasn't clear in her head how all of the people fitted together. Smoothing out her knitting pattern, she began to draw the Blake family tree in a blank corner.

From 1911 Census

SERVANTS - From 1911 Census

ELIZABETH CASTLE (Housemaid)
b. 1892   19 in 1911
(m.? / d.?)

MARGARET SALMON (Cook)
b. 1873
(m?/d?) 38 in 1911

THE BLAKE FAMILY

ANGUS BLAKE
Richard's Great-grandfather
b. 1857 – d.?
m ?

|

JAMES BLAKE
Richard's Grandfather
b. 1885 – d.?
m. Dorothy née ?

|

RONALD BLAKE
Richard's father
b.? – d. 1969
m?

|

RICHARD BLAKE   CORDELIA BLAKE
b. 1934 – d. 1977 age 43   b. 1953 – d?
m. Coral née Wakefield, 1970

|

JAMES BLAKE
b. 1971 –
m. Laura Peters, 2003

33

Coral looked around the room and covered her work with her knitting, scared that one of the ghosts might be watching her. Richard would be horrified if he found out that she was nosing into his family history. He would see it as treading very heavily on his toes. Although there was still so much missing, at the very least it made the generations of Richard's family clear. She was shocked she didn't know anything about Richard's mother, not even her name. Thinking back to the photograph on the history website, she hadn't been in it, so she must have died or left the family between Cordelia's birth in 1953 and when the photograph was taken in 1958.

A few days later Coral received another email from Mr Marchant.

RE: ENQUIRY

Dear Coral (if I might be so bold),

I hope you are keeping well. I very much enjoyed our phone conversation last week and appreciate you sending me the Blake family tree you created. There is so much to discuss! This is quite the rum adventure isn't it, digging around in the family's past?

I've found some more documents about the history of the house and the Blake family. It's interesting and curious stuff.

Obviously, there is no access to the census after 1911, but there is a birth certificate and adoption papers for a Beth Castle. Beth was born in 1912 and is registered as the daughter of Elizabeth Castle, father unknown. During the same year, Richard's grandparents, James and Dorothy Blake, adopted Beth. Unfortunately, there is a death certificate for Elizabeth, so she must have died in or sometime after childbirth.

It's actually quite an incredible story – a well-to-do middle class family adopting the child of a servant. They must have been incredibly generous and open-minded for the period. Ronald, Richard's father, was born in 1905 and would have been seven when Beth came to live with them, so it's likely Beth and Ronald would have been brought up as brother and sister. The same year Angus, Richard's great-grandfather died of a heart attack.

Isn't history fun! I'll definitely keep looking for more information and keep you informed.

I hate to pester, but have you yet made your promised donation to St George's?

Kind regards,

Malcolm Marchant.

Local Architectural Historian

Coral updated the information on her family tree. Mr Marchant was right: it was incredible that the family had adopted Elizabeth's fatherless child, although Richard had always been so kind to her that she wasn't surprised that his grandparents had been equally kind.

from 1911 Census,
updated

ELIZABETH CASTLE (Housemaid)
b. 1892 - d.1912, childbirth
m.?

BETH CASTLE
b. 1912, Adopted 1912
(m. ? / d. ?)
Father unknown

THE BLAKE FAMILY

ANGUS BLAKE
Richard's Great-grandfather
b. 1857 — d. 1912
m ?

|

JAMES BLAKE
Richard's Grandfather
b. 1885 — d.?
m. Dorothy née ?

|

RONALD BLAKE
Richard's father
b. 1905 — d. 1969
m ?

RICHARD BLAKE
b. 1934 - d. 1977 age 43
m. Coral née Wakefield, 1970

|

JAMES BLAKE
b. 1971 —
m. Laura Peters, 2003

CORDELIA BLAKE
b. 1953 - d.?

Mr Marchant also hadn't made it clear if Elizabeth had died in the house, but Coral wasn't sure if that was crucial. Her ghost may still be able to appear in the house even if she died in a hospital. It was not as if there was a set of rules she could consult, like she did when she was at secretarial college. Besides, it didn't answer the question of who The Slender Man could be. A servant, or maybe James, Richard's grandfather, were possibilities. It was strange to think why he would adopt a fatherless child if he had been so cruel to the mother in her lifetime.

Coral hadn't been expecting a parcel, but always enjoyed receiving them, especially a surprise. She peered into the padded envelope. It was a book. Her first thought was that Agnes, her friend from book club, had sent her the latest novel on the reading list. She pulled it out and looked at the cover: 'Understanding History'. It seemed to be an introduction to historical research. She opened the cover and there was a dedication written in bold black ink – *Wonderful to have found a fellow historian. Here's to the past and the future. Malcolm Marchant.* This was a generous sentiment and she was grateful for it, but she wasn't trying to understand history – only what was going on in her house. History lessons wouldn't give her any tips on how to speak with her ghosts.

*****

"Don't be afraid. You can tell me all about it. I can help you. Richard can help you." Coral wandered around the house at all times of the day and night, calling out in every room, waiting a few minutes and then moving on to the next. Her frustration increased with each day of silence.

"Please. Where are you? Either of you." Coral hummed the girl's tune, hoping she'd be able to hear and understand she cared for her.

"I haven't heard that tune since Dad died." James was standing in the doorway of the living room. His mother had her back to him, unaware of his presence. He approached and laid his hand on her shoulder. She slowly awoke from her trance and stared at him for a moment as if she didn't recognise him.

"Oh, James, I didn't hear you come in."

"Evidently. What's all this about? I thought we were past this a long time ago." Coral stared at him, confused at what he could mean.

"I know there's something wrong. It's like after Dad died. You're not really here." With a gentle grasp he held onto the tops of her arms and bobbed his head down to look into her eyes.

"How could you know, you were just a child." Coral was angry and unlike herself. James released her, sighing with the weight of misunderstanding.

"How would you know, you were just a zombie."
He continued, "Look Mum, you're tired, you look
terrible. Come and stay with me for a while."

"I miss him, James. It never goes away."

*****

James would be here soon. Such a long time had
passed without incident that she felt able to leave
for a few days in any case. She checked herself in
her dressing table mirror and picked up a pair of
thin gloves. The feeling of pulling on the well-fitted
gloves was satisfying and completed her dressing. She
would make one more round of the house to check
everything was in order and then she would be ready.
The family tree had helped her to understand some
of the Blakes' history, but there was still something
missing. Coral hoped that whatever was in the safe
would answer some of the questions she still had,
and she'd have to wait for that. It was fine to leave
just for a while until the locksmith got back to her.
The doorbell rang. She wondered why James wasn't
using his keys, he usually did.

As she approached the bedroom door she saw
it again. A feeling of exhilaration flooded through

her, as if she'd seen a destructive lover after a hard-fought separation. She prayed for it to be Richard and reached out her hand and flicked the switch.

The girl was standing with her back to her, in front of the bed. She was wearing a long, white cotton nightdress. Kneeling down the girl began to pray. Her head was bowed, resting on her intertwined hands. Coral watched. This time the scene was clear and without shadows, every detail of the room visible. It thrilled Coral to know that she was getting closer to the girl's reality.

The girl's room was bare except for a brass bed, a set of wooden drawers and a dressing table. Only a brush and washbasin sat on the surface. The wooden floorboards were polished and a large rug in dark colours was laid out before the bed on which the girl knelt. Although the room was austere, the furniture was Edwardian in style and obviously expensive, like the type kept in 'best' rooms when Coral was a child. It was strange that a servant's room should contain such good furniture, and this wasn't the attic room either. Elizabeth may have been allowed to live amongst the family; everything else about their arrangements was odd so it didn't surprise her.

Without showing any signs of being disturbed, the girl remained in position as The Slender Man entered the room and stood behind her. He waited. Coral couldn't see his face and couldn't understand what he was doing. There were no chores for him to correct. As she watched, she became frightened. His patient stillness was disturbing. His shoulders sloped forward, giving the impression he was hunting, greedy to devour her. There was something familiar in the way he stood. He could have been any age but seemed old and worn, as if he'd already lived a long and weary life.

He reached out a hand and stroked her hair, his touch gentle as it glided over her head. The girl froze, fixed in her prayer position, and the muscles of her frame tensed stiff. Still The Slender Man stroked her hair gently, running his fingers down her braid. With no warning at all, he made a sudden move. He pushed his hand down on her head and clamped her into place. Coral understood.

"Elizabeth!!" she shouted. The Slender Man turned his head at the sound, but Coral had already flicked the switch.

"I found these on your doorstep." James held out a generous bunch of spring flowers, a note tucked between the blossoms. Coral stared at the bouquet, and then at her son.

"I'm not coming."

"You're not coming?" James stared at his mother. Her stern gaze reassured him that she meant it, her gentle nature abandoned.

"I have to stay."

"What do you mean, 'have to'? No such thing."

"I'm waiting, James."

"Waiting? What for? Christmas?"

"I think he's here. There's so much he needs to tell me," she whispered.

"Who? Mum, what the ... and we've gone to so much trouble. Laura's made up the spare room and everything."

Coral smiled. "Well, now you won't have to go to any more. Give the flowers to Laura."

James had been angry and reluctant to leave her, but he didn't understand what she had to do. The Slender Man could hear her. That meant the girl could too. She would ask her if there was anything she could do. It might help the girl to know someone cared and wanted to help. Coral could find where in the girl's own time she could go for help. Mr Marchant might know that. The scene had been so solid that maybe it was even possible for the girl to come to the present. Coral wished there was someone she could talk to. She felt sure that Richard would know, but where was he? Instead she was stuck making notes and exploring history with Malcolm Marchant – how far that would get her, she didn't know.

*****

It had taken the locksmith longer than expected to open the safe. The letters found inside were those of James Blake Sr to his son Ronald Blake, Richard's father. More secrets Richard had kept from her. How much he'd known about the birth of his great-aunt Beth, she wasn't sure, but now it was obvious that he had chosen to keep it all from her. The letters were friendly and kind, the type a parent sends to his son in boarding school and then university. One letter in particular solved the riddle of Beth's adoption. It was dated December 1933.

> *Dearest Ronald,*
>
> *It is with much regret that I have to impress on you the gravity of the situation in which you now find yourself. I do not expect you to understand only to accept what I tell you. We all love Beth, she is a beautiful and charming daughter and sister, but a sister is all she can be to you. My father was a loving father and I never suffered at his hand, but he was cruel and cavalier with the servants, especially the young females. Bad blood has been the result and we have made amends as well as we could. Beth has had a happy, fulfilling life.*
>
> *She is to be sent away to finishing school and we*

will find you a suitable wife. It is my and your mother's wish you should be married by the summer and only then will Beth be allowed to return.

Please understand we mean to be kind and save both you and Beth further unnecessary pain.

Your affectionate father.

Coral wanted to be angry with Richard for not telling her, but to confess his own great-grandfather Angus had been so cruel and depraved would have been hard. At least his grandfather, James, had made up for it. No wonder Richard had insisted his own son be named after him. Poor Elizabeth, she must have suffered a great deal, being raped by her employer and dying soon after the birth of her child, Beth. It made Coral more determined to help her rest in peace.

Again Coral waited. The uncertainty of her vigil made her hypersensitive to every noise in the house. At night, the inevitable creaks and hums that take centre stage resounded in her head, amplified and mingled with her confused thoughts. Elizabeth had died, but what about Beth, mother and daughter both mixed up in the Blake family. Information was missing. Often she would hear a sound, which sent her running around the house searching for its source, her hope that it would be a prelude to the switch held tight in her chest. Her exhaustion from disappointment and physical exertion brought her low, and she would sit in front of the window staring out into the garden, still, watching for hours. The answer machine clicked on:

"Coral, it's Agnes. Why didn't you come to book club? It's a bit rude if you ask me. Call me back and soon."

It clicked again:

"Mum, this is becoming silly. Please call me back. Immediately. Love you." Coral continued to sit. She would call them when she had saved the girl.

It appeared in her bedroom again. The same scene as before played out in front of her: the girl bent over her bed praying. Coral knew she only had a few moments before The Slender Man entered so she had to be quick. Moving towards the bed, she touched the girl on the shoulder. It was solid, the girl was actually real. The girl didn't start but instead she did something entirely unexpected. She turned to look at Coral. Then she smiled. Coral grinned.

"Thank you." The girl's voice was sweet and she was without a doubt speaking directly to Coral. They kept smiling at each other. The girl knew she was trying to help her. Coral was overjoyed that at last she could save her.

"Elizabeth, what do you need me to do?" Coral asked as the girl rose to her feet and walked towards the switch. The girl reached out and put her hand on it. She continued smiling as she turned to look at Coral. The girl was confident and in control, not at all how Coral had imagined she would be. Coral was confused.

"I don't need you to do anything. You've already done everything I've hoped and prayed for all these years." Still smiling, the girl flicked the switch and in that instant she was gone.

Coral looked around the bare room. It was quiet and cold. Her feet were bare and she was wearing a long white cotton nightdress. Shivering, she grabbed for the switch, flicking it on and off, but only the light responded. She ran to the dressing table and looked into the mirror. Staring back at her was the girl. The door opened and there stood The Slender Man.

"No prayers tonight, Cordelia."

He closed the door. For the first time Coral looked straight at The Slender Man. He was handsome, but his face constantly changed, moving from youth through to middle age. It was an ever-shifting kaleidoscope of ages. It was a face she knew well.

At last Coral understood. She had her wish.

How long she would be trapped with Richard she didn't know – she didn't know if the switch would ever work again. But she did know why he'd never never talked about his deceased sister.

*****

CONDOLENCES

Dear Coral,

I'm sorry to be writing to you under such unfortunate circumstances. It's incredible that once again the house has been destroyed by fire.

Thank you for the copy of that dreadful letter addressed to Ronald about his failed courtship of his aunt Beth. I agree, such a tangled web.

I have further information about the family. It's more sad news, I'm afraid. Richard's great-aunt Beth also died young. She was sent away to finishing school and never returned. Ronald married Richard's mother that same year and Richard was born around the same time as Beth's death. The death certificate states the cause of Beth's death as septicaemia, but from what it isn't clear. It's a curious family history, but it wasn't uncommon for people to die young, even in the 1930s.

As if it wasn't enough, Richard's sister Cordelia took her

own life. She was only sixteen. Richard was her guardian as his father had been living abroad. It must have been a terrible shock for him and for Richard too of course. He never mentioned it, but I suppose it would have been difficult to talk about.

To clarify the family connections, I've added to the family tree to fill in everything we now know. What started as cruelty ended in tragedy; it's quite Dickensian.

If you need any advice on the restoration of the house, I will gladly be of service.

Again, my commiserations. It would be an honour, now that we have untangled the Blake web, if you would consider joining me for dinner? Did you receive the flowers?

Kind Regards,

Malcolm Marchant.

THE BLAKE FAMILY TREE

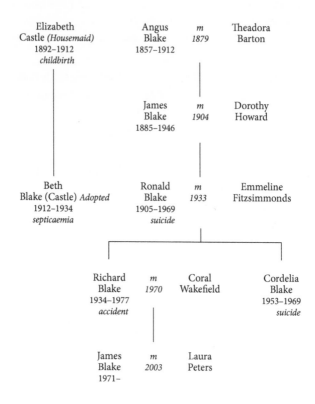

Elizabeth
Castle *(Housemaid)*
1892–1912
childbirth

Angus
Blake
1857–1912

m
1879

Theadora
Barton

James
Blake
1885–1946

m
1904

Dorothy
Howard

Beth
Blake (Castle) *Adopted*
1912–1934
septicaemia

Ronald
Blake
1905–1969
suicide

m
1933

Emmeline
Fitzsimmonds

Richard
Blake
1934–1977
accident

m
1970

Coral
Wakefield

Cordelia
Blake
1953–1969
suicide

James
Blake
1971–

m
2003

Laura
Peters

RE: CONDOLENCES

Dear Mr Marchant,

Thank you for your kindness, but I will not be restoring the house and intend to sell it as it is. I was trapped in that house for too long and it's time for a new life.

As for the sad news, I appreciate your time, but as the house is gone, there is no need to relive the past over and over again. Let it be buried.

Please let me know if you have any interest in buying the house.

I have posted a cheque for £5000 as a contribution to your work. I trust this will be of some use to you.

Yours truly,

Ms C. Blake

Cordelia stopped writing and looked at herself in the mirror. She was sixteen when she had last seen herself. It would take time to get used to an old face but at least Coral had looked good for her age. Looks, however, were not Cordelia's main concern; she had missed too much of life.

She'd always felt sorry for her father, Ronald, but Mr Marchant's family tree wasn't entirely accurate. Ronald hadn't known Beth was his aunt when he fell in love with her, nor had Beth known when she accepted his love. But he and his new wife had accepted their baby, Richard, despite his 'bad blood', poor Beth having died from complications after the birth. Ronald could never have predicted how much Richard would take after his great-grandfather, Angus. When he did find out it was too late – Cordelia was gone. Ronald challenged Richard and, furious at being discovered, Richard murdered Ronald by locking him in the house and starting the fire.

Ronald had failed to protect her, and Cordelia had been desperate enough to kill herself. She regretted it. If she had known what purgatory was like, she would never have done it. Years trapped in the house, repeatedly hearing her father's screams as he tried to escape the fire, and then after Richard's death, his return to torment her. Her punishment had been cruel and relentless. It didn't matter now though. It was over. She had dwelt long enough with all of their pasts.

She shut the lid of the computer. It hadn't taken her long to understand the rudiments of modern technology and this was now the world in which she lived. And living was what she intended to do.

The Pier

The girl's hair was being blown in three directions. Her coat, unfastened and loose, revealed a red spotted dress; the thin fabric alternately pressed against the front and then the back of her body, outlining her skinny legs. Grasping the top rung of the rail she stepped onto the lowest, her red Wellington boot slipping as she positioned herself, locking her outstretched arms and leaning her body backwards. The sea leapt up, spray merging with the rain spitting onto her fragile face.

Why don't they stop her? Good lord, I can't look. Some parents are so irresponsible.

Anna had been watching the family for a while. Safe in the end-of-pier café, she held her Earl Grey tea in both hands, enjoying its warmth, inhaling the fragrant steam. On the beach red, green, blue and yellow huts clung together shrouded in grey. A teenager in the guise of a waitress stopped behind her. As she bent over Anna's shoulder, her fringe fell in front of her eyes. Flicking it back, she dropped a plate onto the tabletop. It clanked then bounced as it made contact with the veneered surface.

"Thank you," Anna said.

She tried to catch the waitress's attention, her wide smile making visible the extent of her gratitude. The waitress didn't look, retreating beyond a cluster of empty tables. Anna concentrated her attention upon the new arrival. Coffee and walnut cake, her favourite. Wind threw rain against the window, the interior edges were decorated with condensation, acting as a substitute net curtain. The girl's parents looked carefree, or careless, laughing as the wind harassed them, roughing them up. They stood defiant, their legs wide, arms held up, as if suspended starfish. Waves battered the pale-blue Victorian structure. It remained stoic.

It's fine for them, they're grown-ups, they can make their own decisions, but that child ... well, really. Oh my god!

Anna grasped at her chest as the child pulled herself level with the rail then hung forward over it, looking directly at the dark mutating water surface. They shouldn't let her climb on the rail like that, she could be ... Anna didn't want to think it. She'd never let her child do that.

The door opened. Wind took possession of it, forcing it back and forth, a freezing gust penetrating the room. It lifted defenceless napkins from the tables and knocked over condiments before it was denied access by the teenage waitress as she slammed the door shut.

"Come on love, sit down. I'll get you a cuppa." The moon-faced older waitress behind the counter chirped at the old man. He didn't look up as he shuffled his way past the tables in front of her.

"Filthy day," she continued to his back. He nodded, and dragged a straight-backed wooden chair from its place underneath a table. The waitress placed a tray, set with tea things, in front of him. Generous portions of cream and jam occupied two small pots. A plate piled with scones nestled beside them.

"There you go, love." The waitress winked at him. He took hold of her hand and patted it.

"No need to thank me, I know you'd do the same for me." She smiled, returned to her original position behind the cash desk, and picking up a thick novel, she continued to read.

Anna wondered what it would take to get that kind of attention. She'd been coming here for a long time and didn't know how much longer was required. Maybe she didn't look lonely enough. Or old enough. The man had oversized sagging earlobes, the remainders of his white hair clung to the back of his freckle-infested head. Did *he* have any children?

The girl laughed as the wind, without any consideration for common decency, raised her skirt into the air, momentarily revealing her undergarments. It reminded Anna of a holiday she'd taken, at least five years ago. Before the rape anyway. As she had stood with her husband on the platform of Marseille train station, a huge gust of warm, humid air had blown the skirt of a teenager high above her slender hips.

"Ooh la la!" the girl had shouted. And they'd laughed about it for a long time, disbelieving that a French person would use such a phrase. (They'd considered cliché a cultural myth; used only to stereotype and categorise something unknown.) It had become one of their jokes.

I suppose they know what they're doing, it's not really my business.

She wondered how she would feel if some busy-body had told her how to raise her child, externally assessing the risk of her family outings. She'd never know. That decision had been taken away from her when she'd miscarried after the attack. Her own child would now be about the same age as the girl.

Anna's attention was diverted to the old man, who stuffed a large piece of scone covered with cream and jam into his mouth. A large blob of the mingled substances fell onto the plate. He ignored it and continued pushing the sweet treat into his tortoise-like mouth.

The sponge and cream fought to be the first through the prongs as Anna pressed the fork down into the thin end of her cake. Pulling the fork carefully away and turning it upside down she wiped it onto her tongue. She sucked on the cake, enjoying the feel of it in her mouth. It was sweet then bitter. She lived for small pleasures. Pleasures she'd taken a long time to give herself permission for. Her husband had never been willing to get to this stage. As far as he was concerned she was spoilt goods. No amount of time, he'd said, could change that for him. She'd lost her baby, her husband, and without him, the chance of motherhood. The irony of his reaction had overwhelmed her; it was a cliché he'd used to distance *her* as unknown and terrifying.

"Oh sweetheart, you're taking London to the seaside. We'll miss you, but I'm sure you'll be so calm and creative there," her mother had said.

And so she'd gone ... It hadn't been the most practical solution, but that wasn't the point. Her freelance work had been going well; she'd had two commissions to illustrate children's books and had sold a variety of pictures. Her city life was full with meetings, dinner parties and gallery trips. It was all she'd imagined for herself as an art student. After her husband left she really believed the move to the seaside would help her to get over the attack.

People found it easy to be there for her at first, but as time passed and daily life intervened – their daily lives – people forgot and left her to herself. Especially when their own offspring arrived.

"You know how it is. Everything's so much harder with a little one in tow," her sister had said. She imagined it must be. Anna hadn't told anyone she'd been pregnant.

Anna stuck her fork into the remaining piece of cake. It was hard. She pulled the fork out and placed it onto the table, staring at the uneaten half of her slice. She thought she'd like to ask for a new piece, but they might think her greedy, or worse, that she was making a fuss. The old man wiped the crumbs from his face with the sleeve of his worn, grey cardigan. He's old, he doesn't count, he can eat what he likes. *Come on, Anna, just ask. What's the worst that could happen?*

"Excuse me." Anna partially stood up. Her chair screeched. The young waitress dragged herself up from her stool, her thin shoulders slumped forward, her feet slapping on the ground as she approached.

"I'm very sorry, but this cake, it's a bit stale." Anna laughed, avoiding eye contact with the girl. "On the crust."

The girl leant on one hip and shrugged.

"Could I get a fresh piece?" Anna tried to look

directly at the girl but failed.

"Erm, please," she added.

"Manda, is that all right?" The girl looked to her companion behind the cash desk.

"What, love?" She looked up from her book.

"A new bit of cake, this one's stale, she says." The girl had a loud voice.

The old man looked up from his scone and turned to observe Anna.

"Has she eaten it?"

"Half." The waitress snorted. Manda laughed.

"It can't have been that bad."

Anna's skin burnt. The waitress snatched the plate away and retraced her path across the café. The girl ran side to side across the end of the pier, jumping in the puddles that had formed in the grooves of the worn surface. Giggling as she squatted, placing her hands spread to their full size into the shallow pools. Once again she ran to the edge and plopped down, hanging her knotted-cotton legs over the side of the platform, her shiny boots dangling from the ends of them. Anna wanted to go to her, bring her inside, buy her cake and hot chocolate, make her warm and dry. That's what her parents should do.

What do they think they're doing?

The couple finished kissing, pulling away from each other, shielded in their matching yellow cagoules.

They don't even pay her any attention.

A wave crashed next to the couple, the water covering their feet. Jumping back, they laughed again, shaking their sodden boots. They did, at least, all look like they were having fun.

The second piece of cake was perfect: moist, creamy and sweet. She ate it with speed, concentrating on each mouthful, absorbed by the rhythm of lifting it to her mouth and chewing.

"Anna darling, if the sea air doesn't suit you anymore, why don't you come back to London, stay in our spare room to start with? It would be so much easier all round."

Her sister didn't understand. She'd had four children by the time she was thirty. Of course it would be convenient for her, knowing that Anna could provide free regular childcare. After all, what did she fill her time with?

Anna thought about the two men who had taken her life from her. She saw them both in her dreams, mutated into one. Sometimes she saw the man in dark clothes step out in front of her, blocking her way, his face hidden. As he approached, she saw it was her husband. She tried to talk to him, to calm him down, but he wouldn't speak. Panicking, she tried to run, only to wake up alone, glad he was no longer there. Relief faded, replaced by the knowledge she'd failed. It was her fault he'd never been caught. She'd been asked repeatedly for her attacker's description, but couldn't remember what he looked like. Her husband had withdrawn entirely; she'd never anticipated how easy it could be for him to be so cold.

They could at least button her coat up. She's soaked through. The girl's hands were exposed, raw, glowing red. Rain had outdone the wind, water dripped from the ends of her saturated hair.

Really, this is too much. She should go and say something to the couple.

Surely it's not interfering if it's for the good?

The girl was fearless. She played with the wind and rain, enjoying all that it summoned. Anna was like that herself as a child. She had pretended to get annoyed at the way her mother fussed about her in all weathers; was she too hot, too cold, were her feet wet, was her head covered? She'd hated the wind but hated the constraint of wearing a hat more. But her mother would force one on her head and pull it down over her ears.

"You'll be back crying with earache if you don't keep it on."

She loved the way her mother was right. It made her feel protected. Being protected made her fearless.

Anna wanted to go to the toilet, but somehow felt if she gave up her vigil, even for the short time it would take for a trip to the loo, she would be abandoning the child. All the while she was there she felt the child would be safe. Three cups of Earl Grey made her reconsider.

When she returned, her tea things had gone, and so had the family. She was relieved. The rain was now a dense mass of grey obscuring her vision, the sea and sky indistinguishable from one another. Anna placed the exact money needed to pay the bill on the plate and dressed herself for the outside. The old man was now licking the last remaining globules of mixed up jam and cream from his plate, his tongue, fat and wet, dragged across the surface. Anna picked up her bag and umbrella and darted towards the door.

Manda called out after her:

"Bye, love. See you again."

Anna kept her head down and jerked her arm up. The young waitress mumbled goodbye without looking up.

Anna walked along the seafront, marching quickly against the wind, her umbrella rebelling, colluding with the wind, springing one way and then another. The couple were walking on the other side of the street, linking arms, close into each other. Anna looked for their child; she wasn't there. Hesitating for only a second, Anna crossed the street and approached them.

"Your little girl ... I'll help you find her." The couple looked at her, then at one another. They giggled with shock.

"I'm sorry, we don't have a little girl. We don't have any children. Not yet anyway ..." Anna was confused.

"I'm sorry ... I saw you on the pier ... that child." She stopped, and looked around her, the wind pushing her from all sides. The young man touched her on the arm. She flinched, stepping back.

"Which child?" He frowned, then half smiled.

They walked on, looking back at her and giving a brief wave. Their heads closed together.

Anna turned towards the pier. Waves still crashed against it, but it would not be moved. She stood staring for a minute. Dropping her umbrella she ran along the seafront to the pier. The rain thrashed against her, soaking her hair until it was sodden, and the wind pushed into her, fighting to hold her back. As she ran towards the end of the pier, a wave broke over the railings in front of her. The shock made her laugh. Circling the cluster of empty shops that stood in the centre of the pier, she was exhilarated as the wind battered her from all sides, her hair and clothes pushed and pulled. Looking out to sea, in the arcade and under the shelters, she ran up and down searching for the girl. Her exhilaration made her as fearless as when she'd been young, when she knew her mother was always there for her.

At the end-of-pier café both waitresses were watching her through the window, their frowns of confusion visible through the misty panes of glass. The moon-faced waitress opened the door and shouted, "Get yourself in here. You'll catch your death."

Anna half ran towards her. Instinctively, she took the waitress's hands, trying to drag her outside.

"The little girl, the one playing here before, she's gone. We must find her."

"Which little girl? There's only been you, that mad couple in yellow and Frank here all morning. Come in." She was stern.

Anna stood for a moment, confused. She looked behind her, the pier was deserted.

"But …"

The waitress had already moved inside. Anna followed wanting to protest. A fluffy cream towel was held out to her.

"Dry yourself off, love. I'll make you some tea."

Anna rubbed the towel over her dripping head and raw face. She removed her coat and hung it on a brass hook next to the door. Her hands were freezing, but at least her feet were dry. She smiled as she slipped her sacred red Wellington boots from her thin calves, warming her feet against the radiator. The girl was free to roam but she would always be in her, giving her the reassurance she needed to be fearless.

Tomorrow, Anna decided, she would ring her sister, to ask if her spare room back in London was still available.

LAST POST

The old man sat in the communal lounge. Light from the large window created a distorted square, stretching across the deep green carpet. Otherwise, the room was gloomy and stark. George stared through the window. Grey cloud covered the sky and a faint outline of the sun was barely visible, its rays fighting their way through. The spidery fingers of bare tree branches waved to him as the wind forced them up and down. He longed to inhale the smell of damp earth.

It made him think of the boy. He wondered whether he'd be in an old people's home too, unable to care for himself. On the afternoon the boy first came to him, it had been warm and bright. The orchard was alight – sunrays dodged the leaves on the apple trees and touched the grass in changing formations. A warm breeze made the tree branches shiver. George took the boy's outstretched fingers, allowing himself to be led, going deeper amongst the trees.

"*Reste ici,*" he said, and pushed George towards a tree.

George had relived every moment, trying to re-member if he'd given the boy any cause to be that confident. At the time though he'd simply retreated, stepping backwards until he was stopped, his back against the tree. The boy kissed him. Moving his hands, he'd placed them onto George's body. George closed his eyes and kissed him back.

"George, George – are you okay?" He opened his eyes and George saw the boy, his thick, blond hair backlit and glowing, giving him a halo. He was beautiful. But this was not his boy. George felt ashamed, caught out by his reminiscences.

"What do you want?"

"No need to bark, dear. You need to fill in your menu. I'll just pop it down here, you can do it when you're ready."

George stared up at the carer. His unguarded smile glistened with lip gloss and the glitter smeared around his eyes made George uncomfortable. He despised flamboyance. The heavy jewel-encrusted cross that hung from his neck had to be a joke. He couldn't believe in God, being the way he was.

"I want some tea," George said.

"Okey-dokey." Gabriel crossed the room, his walk feminine and mannered. He twisted on the balls of his feet before disappearing through the door of the common-room kitchen. He'd only been working at the home a few weeks, but he'd conjured memories George had wrestled to suppress.

*****

George was nineteen in 1944 and D-day was only the second action he'd seen. He'd been frightened, they all were, not that they'd admit it. He was already engaged to Iris; they'd made the announcement while he was on his last leave. George thought she was pretty, but it was her fierce humour and bossy streak that he loved.

His battalion was lucky enough to be billeted at a farm, sleeping in one of the barns. When the men arrived they'd been exhausted, dirty and some blood-soaked. Being freed from occupation had gone to the locals' heads and they were generous in their gratitude. Johnny, the farmer, sent one of the farm hands with bread, cheese and wine. The young man stared directly at George without smiling. His gold hair was a striking contrast to his black eyes. Tanned and healthy, he made the squaddies look as pale and greasy as uncooked sausages. George was disquieted by his sullen beauty and self-assurance.

Those first few days, George was like a cat on hot bricks. He tried to believe it was because he was recovering from action and missing the friends they'd lost. He wrote to Iris telling her he was safe, that farm life was a shock; it was hard work and smelt bad. George told her he couldn't wait to come home and marry her. But he wandered around the farmyard, hoping for a glimpse of the boy. He wasn't even sure why he was so desperate to see him. It was only a short time before George was being led into the orchard.

After that afternoon many encounters followed. Whenever there was a chance to get away, they took it. Initially, the boy came to him, coaxing him to follow. But soon, George sought the boy out, taking him by surprise at his chores and leading him to a new hiding place. George was sick and confused. He'd had no idea he was capable of doing such things. He'd never even seen a woman naked. George told himself it was the war that led him to do these things, things that both excited and disgusted him.

Returning to the barn late one afternoon, the other lads were already playing cards, or lounging across the bales of hay. Mitchel had noticed his absences.

"Missed you this afternoon, George. Too good to shovel shit are you?" George felt sick.

"Johnny just wanted me to help with the milking. They're a hand short." He was curt.

"So you lent a hand, or put your hand to good use more like and gave yourself a good milking." Mitchel pretended to pleasure himself. They all laughed. George barked a laugh too, but skulked off to the back of the barn and climbed to the top of the haystack.

"He wants to be alone, can't get enough," Mitchel shouted after him. Again, they all laughed. Anger leapt from his fear – he wanted to rip Mitchel's head off. George knew the consequences if he were ever found out. Ridiculed. Bullied. Shamed and ostracised. A dread of discovery now clung to George. But Mitchel was right; he couldn't get enough. He withdrew from the others, and buried his desires deep from view. His aggression he wore on his sleeve and if anyone dared make suggestions about his habits again, he'd be sure to beat their curiosity out of them.

The affair lasted only a few weeks until they were moved on. George was devastated to be going, but his relief was just as great. He was shattered by the experience and locked it away; intense love, crippling grief and self-loathing had exhausted him.

On his wedding night, George knew that as the man he was expected to take control, but he didn't know what to do. This was his chance to rescue the happy-go-lucky boy that had gone to France. Iris had already undressed and lay under the bedclothes. He flicked off the light, slipped off his underwear and quickly got into the bed, lying next to her. He hesitated, but Iris prompted him.

"Go on then." She giggled. It made him laugh and that broke the tension. He felt, at least, they were in it together. So he kissed her, their lips dry and closed, her body soft and yielding. He remembered the hard kisses of the boy and his rough lovemaking. Then it was over. He promised Iris it would be better next time. She smiled:

"We can't expect to get it right first time." And they did have plenty of time to get it right, in the proper way. They were married for sixty-two years and he never told her about the boy, and was never unfaithful again. He had chosen a normal life.

*****

Gabe returned holding out a jade cup and saucer, his smile wide. He was so outlandish it was infuriating. Gabe's arms were covered with tattoos of angels which disappeared into the tops of his t-shirt sleeves, as if ascending to Heaven. Only God knew what hid beneath the rest of his outfit. He spoke too loudly with an affected shout, making sure everyone could hear him.

"You're just like me, you like it strong." Gabe laughed as he bent forward to put the cup down.

"No, not there, put it there." George's bony finger

jabbed at the edge of the coffee table to his right.
"Where I can reach it. When's Emily coming?"

"After lunch, George. She'll be here by two-thirty.
It must be wonderful to have a daughter. I'd just
adore it. We could swap make-up tips and notes on
boyfriends," Gabe giggled. A queer having a child
was just against nature, disgusting, George thought.
If he'd been a younger man, he'd take him by the
throat and squeeze. He imagined Gabe's slender
neck in his hands. George looked down at his old
fists: they trembled. He was so pathetic he wouldn't
even be able to kill a fairy.

Iris had died only a few weeks ago, and his
daughter Emily had started to visit more often. He
was bitter that it had taken Iris's death to make her
come. William never came, he lived abroad. George
couldn't understand why, but he respected his inde-
pendence. He glared at his compatriots. Gabe was
making them laugh. He pretended to tip-toe up to a
lady who snoozed, then gently pulled the thin blanket
over her knees. He stood behind some others who
huddled around a glowing television set.

"Oooh, he's so handsome. If only." He laughed
aloud and the others laughed along. A man who
read, raised his eyes as if peering over imaginary
half-moon spectacles. Gabe mouthed an apology,
and continued to tip-toe across the room. They all
loved him, but George could see through his easy

charm and tricks.

Iris had read to the family on cold Sunday afternoons when they hadn't wanted to step out. Her low, steady voice rarely faltered. George became impatient when Emily would interrupt with continual questions: "How long 'til they find the dragon?" or "Why did it need so much gold?" He would reassure her that if only she listened, she'd find out, that's how stories worked. But Emily acted as if she didn't believe him. William never interrupted; he was always so sure of himself, even as a child. The clanking of cooking pots jolted him back to his present and the smells of unidentifiable foods combined to a sour whole as it invaded the dayroom.

"Your beautiful Emily's here," Gabe sang. As he approached, the room brightened. Emily followed, running to catch him up.

"I'll leave you to it. I love the way you do your hair, really suits you," Gabe said to her. Emily, surprised by his comment, blushed. He smiled, gave her a wink and walked away, squeaking on his rubber soles. George wanted to slash at his face and destroy his charming smile. There wasn't anything interesting about Emily's hair. Another lie just to get in her good books.

"Alright Dad?" She bent down and gave him a peck on the cheek. "I don't think we'll read today. I want to talk." Emily had started to cry as she spoke.

Already. It seemed all she'd done since Iris had died. George sulked. He wanted her to read; he didn't want to talk. Emily tried to smile, waiting for her opportunity to speak, twisting a damp tissue into points between her fingers. George looked at her sidelong. Her expectant gaze was both soothing and intrusive. It reminded him of the look Iris gave him when he lied about a broken dish or one pint too many. Iris would listen as he concocted some outlandish fable before cocking a wry eye at him that said, *that's not even remotely persuasive, you can do better than that.* It was possible Emily had found him out and was just waiting for his confession.

"Get on with it then. And stop crying." She sobbed harder.

"I know William's always been your favourite, and now Mum's gone, I'm leaving too."

George stared at her, his lips pushed tight together. It was true, he'd always preferred William and it had taken Iris five years to convince him they should have a second child. She'd asked so very little from him. It was a fair deal.

Emily couldn't leave. Where she would possibly go, George couldn't imagine. He'd never taken the family abroad, he was too scared and had clung to all that was familiar to be safe.

"I want to travel while I still can. First I'll go and visit William in America and then I'll go through

South America."

"You can't leave me here with him." He gestured in the direction of Gabe. He lowered his voice. "And them." He glared at the old people sharing the common room.

Emily stood up and suppressed another sob. "I won't look after you. I can't. I'm not Mum." She opened her bag, pulled out a letter and held it out to him. "This is from Mum. She told me to give it to you once she'd gone."

George looked at it but didn't take it. Emily placed it on the table next to him, blew her nose on her disintegrating tissue and left.

When he raised his head, he was alone. The room was empty and almost dark. George was bewildered. Emily had been resentful but not wrong. He did love her though, just not in the same way as William. William was vital and strong. As he'd grown up, he'd had plenty of friends and there was always a girl on his arm. George liked that. Emily lived in her imagination, making up stories and inserting drama into everyday events until a simple excursion became an adventure fraught with danger. He was a little wary of her. She would come to them with her crumpled notebook in hand, wanting an audience for her fiction. Well, it was Iris's job to listen to her nonsense as far as he was concerned. It wasn't healthy to live in your head, making all sorts of things up. He was thirsty and hoped his tea was still on the table next to him, but the small blue envelope had replaced it.

Iris had loved to write letters. She seemed to know so many people he'd never met, some even in America. He would watch her, her small head bowed, silhouetted against the light, holding her fountain pen, concentrating and calmly forming letters on the page. He'd not known what she was telling all these people. When he'd asked her, she'd smiled and said, bits and bobs, the children and church, and the weather. He had failed to see how that could be interesting to anyone, but it pleased Iris. When she'd finished, they would stroll to the post office together and he'd relished her look of satisfaction as she pushed the letters into the mouth of the red postbox.

George never wrote letters and dreaded receiving them. Communication could bring unwanted news. When he had received the letter he'd long been dreading, he'd decided he must put an end to his anxiety. If the boy ever came to England and started blabbing his mouth off, his hard-fought peace would be over. George would never let that happen.

Knowing what he had to do didn't worry him. It thrilled George to practice holding his knife, ready to attack, cutting the blade through the air in different directions to see which would be the most effective. He fantasised about pushing the blade into the boy's stomach, slicing through his flesh. He told Iris he was going away for a few nights to meet with some old army friends, packed a small bag and slipped his switchblade into his sock.

But the boy had become a handsome man in his 30s, with a young family, all as healthy and vibrant as him. George was welcomed into their home as an honoured guest, the hero of the liberation. He treated George like a long-lost friend and betrayed no sign of remembering their intimacy. His wife wanted to hear about how George helped to free France and their farm.

Lying in bed that night he waited, his hand grasping the knife under his pillow. When the boy came, he'd be ready to kill him. But he didn't come. George almost wept with relief and disappointment. To the boy, George was little more than a character in a war story told to impress his wife and children. His love had meant nothing. George felt ridiculous, what with his love, the knife and his plan for murder.

Emily was born the following year. Over time George's shame grew into bitterness, and he again fantasised of returning to France to cut the boy's throat. Not from fear, but to teach him that there could be no happy ending. But George well understood he was alone in his rancour and the boy had moved on.

"It's dark in here, George." Gabe clicked on the light. It flickered above until settling to a bright, yellow glare.

"That's better. It's nearly dinnertime, just time for a quick cuppa. I know you love your tea." He laughed. "And I know you like it just there," as he placed a hot cup of tea in the spot George had indicated earlier. Gabe was so smug, he always seemed to know what people needed. A cup of tea, reassurance about their medication, or just a chat. George had overheard the others talking: Gabe was so caring, attentive, an angel heaven sent. They'd even nicknamed him 'The Angel Gabriel'. Angel? George fumed. An interfering fairy, more like. Gabe didn't seem to realize he was there to make beds and wipe arses and not to give spiritual guidance, trying to save their souls. It was too late anyway; if they hadn't made their peace by now there was no hope of change.

Gabe picked up the envelope and read it.

"Don't you want to read your letter?" Gabe

flapped it in front of his face. "Secret lover, George? Never thought you'd be the type."

"Give it here, it's none of your business." George snatched it from Gabe's hands and crushed it into his cardigan pocket.

"When's Emily coming in next? She's so good to come and see her old dad, and you can see how much she misses her mum. It must be hard. For both of you."

"None of your business."

"Oh George, there's nothing wrong with loving your mum. Or your wife come to that. Losing your best friend after all those years, well, I just can't imagine." Gabe half-smiled with sympathy and tenderness. If it wasn't for the lip gloss George might have believed he was sincere.

"You know where I am if you need me." George watched Gabe walk away. Gabe couldn't know anything about his family and all they'd shared. Or – he felt the letter in his pocket – about their secrets.

George switched on his bedside lamp. A triangle of light spread across the pale mustard bedclothes. He retrieved the letter from his cardigan pocket and smoothed out the wrinkles. Iris's handwriting was so familiar; he touched the words in an attempt to understand her. What could she have to say to him? Gabe was right. He did miss her. She was a constant presence, his comfort and security. He had never regretted marrying her; she had provided everything he'd ever wanted, including proof he wasn't a bad person. She had saved him and he was profoundly grateful for her. He longed to read her words and imagine her voice reading them aloud. But the letter must contain something she couldn't tell him when she was alive and there was only one thing that they'd never talked about. His secret. Iris was perceptive, it was obvious she'd found out and stayed only for the children. That would be just like her to put the family first, even if she did despise him. Whatever she knew, he couldn't face it; it was better to live without the certainty. If he didn't know, he could still pretend. He wouldn't read it.

"What are you doing here?" George struggled to sit up in bed. Gabe pulled back the curtains with one swift move. The orange glow of the room transformed into the low glare of daylight.

"Double shift. Sorry love, can't get rid of me that easily. I'll just tidy round and then I'll pop and get your tea." George lay in bed watching Gabe potter around the room. Gabe couldn't be so content being the way he was, George thought. Today his lips were bright pink and his fake lashes long and thick. No one else in the home seemed bothered about the way Gabe was, even some he would have expected to disapprove. He'd won them all over, but George would never accept it. He knew things had changed over the years, the sexual revolution and gay marriage, but it didn't change anything for George. It was still wrong. He didn't care if it made him a bigot; everyone should know where they stand and do their duty. Gabe picked up his letter and inhaled.

"Smells dee-lish. Go on, open it, it can't be that bad," he coaxed. George was furious. He felt as if Gabe could see right through him, see his past sickness. He felt exposed.

"We all have skeletons, George." Gabe gave George a wink as he left the room. What did he mean – he didn't know anything. This boy had come from God knows where, raking up his memories and accusing him of having secrets. George panicked. Gasping for breath, he groped for his inhaler on his bedside cabinet. As he grabbed for it, it fell onto the floor. George couldn't breathe and gulped at the air. He tried to reach forward, but fell hands first onto the ground.

"What on earth is going on here?" Gabe was calm. He put the teacup down, picked up the inhaler, helped George to sit up and held the inhaler to George's mouth. George grabbed at the inhaler and attempted to push Gabe away. Gabe sighed and positioned it back into George's mouth, but George resisted, clasping his wrists and trying to wrestle him, forcing his arms outwards. With ease, Gabe slipped his hands out of George's grasp, collected his wrists into one hand and with the inhaler in the other, he once again placed it into George's mouth.

"Now George, breathe in. One, two, three." Gabe pushed on the inhaler and George breathed, inhaling deep. They both sat for a moment. George was impotent, his pride as thoroughly erased as his strength.

"You can't get out of it that way. Too easy." Gabe laughed. Then he helped George into an armchair and handed him his tea. George stared into his cup. The liquid steamed, and moisture covered the lenses of his glasses.

"I'm pathetic." George was exhausted from fighting, and couldn't explain where these confessional words were coming from, but continued. "And a liar."

Gabe looked at George and smiled, as he transferred his weight from one hip to another. "You, the world and his wife. You need to learn to be kinder to yourself. And cheer up for heaven's sake."

"Are you okay, Dad? I've been worried sick." George watched his daughter half-run towards him. She clasped her unwieldly bag to her chest, her coat hung open.

"I'm fine." He shrugged.

"Funny, you have an attack when I tell you I'm off abroad. And you know I work on Tuesdays." She flopped down in the chair and dropped her bag on the floor.

"I didn't ask you to come." He refused to look at her.

"Gabe said you were upset." Scowling, he turned to look at her.

"If Gabe told you to put your head in an oven …" Emily looked at her father. As he moved something reflected on his face.

"What's that?" She scrutinized him for a moment and smiled.

"What do you mean?" George grunted.

"That on your face, it's sparkling." George's cheek was smothered in glitter. Emily started to laugh at her serious old dad covered in sparkles.

"You look like the Sugar Plum Fairy." George wiped hard at his cheek and stared down at the glitter clinging to his palm. Emily laughed aloud at her father's horror.

"You'll be wearing lipstick next."

Wind thrashed at the trees, banging their branches hard against the window, as if they demanded refuge from the storm. George couldn't sleep. His eyes remained wide open and strained, although his body ached and he longed to let go. He slipped his hand under the pillow and groped for the envelope. Gabe was right. He couldn't avoid it. If he didn't read it, he'd get no peace. George was sure this letter was the end of their marriage. Switching on the light and sitting up, he readied himself. The envelope crackled as he ripped it open, the scent of Iris's perfume merged with the new paper. He sighed deep as he unfolded the single sheet.

Dearest George,

If you're reading this, I've passed on, but won't rest until I tell you what a terrible thing I've done. I lied to you George, William isn't your son. His father is an American GI. When you asked me to marry you I was happy and looking forward to our life together knowing I could love you, and I was sure you felt the same for me. I couldn't complain about you as a husband or a father to William and Emily, and although we didn't say it much, I have always loved you in a way and respected you.

The thought you'd never come back was terrifying. I took a job in the service canteen, where I met Aaron. It only lasted a few weeks, but he begged me

*to go back to America and start a new life with him.
I was tempted. When I knew I was pregnant, I asked
you to come home on leave to be married straight
away. I wanted to pretend you were the baby's father.*

*I'm sorry, George. Over the years I did think about
what my life would have been like in America and I
did keep in contact with Aaron. I sent him pictures of
William throughout the years. Sometimes I wanted to
leave, take the kids and start again. But you were my
best friend, and I never regretted staying, even though
you were not the same George that went off to war.*

*I beg for your kindness and hope you can forgive
me, as I would forgive you.*

*Your affectionate wife,
Iris.*

George's shock almost made him laugh. This
must be his punishment: his beloved son was never
his in the first place. William must have known,
he'd made a fool of him and run off to his real dad
in America as soon as was possible. The people he'd
trusted the most had both lied to him. He'd given
up his French boy for Iris and she'd known how
proud he was of William. That contract he'd made
with her, the children and with life itself – to care
for each other and create a good life – she'd broken
it before he'd even married her. And then broken

it over and over again with every letter she'd sent. He'd lost everything. It gave him twisted pleasure to know they'd both been thwarted lovers and lived with their mutual fear of discovery. George's rage gave his old limbs renewed strength. He picked up the chair next to his bed and threw it to the ground, but it just bounced across the linoleum. He stood seething at his own insignificance and grief.

Gabe stepped into the room and looked at the upturned chair. He raised an eyebrow to reveal the full extent of his peacock eye make-up.

"Now what are you getting up to? You're nothing but trouble you are." He bent down and picked up the chair and returned it to its original position. George had had enough of this snooping queen.

"You bloody fairy. How can you judge me? You don't know me or the mistakes I made."

But his rage slipped away from him. George cried in frustration; his plan for a normal life had failed. "I tried to be good, I tried to make it up to Iris. I wasn't enough of a man and not brave enough to face that truth. Now I have nothing left." George shook and gasped for breath. Gabe handed him his inhaler and rested his arm on his shoulder. George wriggled away from him, sobbing.

"You didn't do anything wrong, George. You may have made some choices that weren't ideal, but you didn't make the worst of choices, thank the Lord."

Gabe clapped his hands together and looked to the sky. George looked at him with disbelief.

"What do you mean?"

"Your French boy. He's still alive and has led a good life. It could have been different if you had followed through with your little plan."

Gabe raised his clenched fist, holding an imaginary knife and moved it forward in a repeated stabbing motion. George's terror again fuelled violence. He lunged forward, his hands outstretched, but Gabe caught hold of his wrists.

"Don't shoot the messenger, George, and we've already learned that killing doesn't solve this problem." He gently placed George's arms by his side and ushered him to sit on the bed. Gabe continued talking.

"You have loved and been loved. You and Iris were the best of friends, you made a good life for one another." George, still out of breath, engulfed by his raging fear, tried to speak.

"William isn't mine. You don't understand, I've lost him and Iris …"

"You've lost nothing. You both kept secrets but from them you two created a life with its own truth. You both loved. Each other. Your children. The life you created together. As Iris says, 'Forgive me, as I would forgive you.'"

George was quiet.

"How about forgiving yourself, George?"

"How can I, I'm not right, I'm ... unnatural."

"Unnatural? Not right? Who is, George? We're all God's creatures. It's not about who you love, but how you love. And you love brilliantly."

George had compensated his entire life for his actions in France, pretending to be good and do the right thing. It served him right that Iris and William had deceived him. He deserved it.

"Forgiveness and love are yours George, just allow yourself to accept them."

The winter sun won its battle and finally broke through the cloud. A wave of light crept across the room. The grey vanquished by gold. Gabe hadn't finished:

"Emily is a wonderful woman and a loyal daughter, George. She loves you and she needs your love."

"Please, just stop crying." George tried to remain patient.

"Are you sure, Dad? It's so much money." Emily stared down at the cheque in her hand, a squashed tissue in the other. She started to speak, but George interrupted her.

"For heaven's sake woman, be quiet. Just remember to let me know where you are and I'll write to you. If you want." She nodded from behind her sodden tissue.

"I'll still be here for you when you get back and I'll want to hear all your stories."

CHERRY

Course I'm speaking to you. Who else do you think I'm gabbing on to? I don't just talk to myself. Then I said to her, "Fucking hell, what does it take to get a cloth over here? I ain't asking for the Crown

Jewels." Then the woman said she had to go, and I thought piss off then, if you really wanna chat then why don't you? We'd just got started. Anyway, I had to be getting off, the bus was due. I did ask her if she fancied meeting again, but she shot off like a whippet. It couldn't have been that nice to meet – lying cow. Shame. I didn't have a chance to tell her how Cherry went away. But I'm sure you don't mind. You're stuck with me now anyway.

The bus is so expensive, I ain't sure how OAPs can afford it. I struggle and I work, and those bloody drivers can be so frigging moody, it's almost like you're invisible sometimes, it really winds me up. I'd like to see 'em crack a smile once in a fucking while. They're so bloody noisy too, juddering and squeaking. The buses, I mean, not the drivers.

That old dear said they got free travel, but she knew exactly what I meant. She wouldn't be able to get out if it weren't for her bus pass. You must have seen her, she's always on the bus, she don't 'alf get about. Says her legs have been on the dodgy side since her operation, but they looked all right to me. I like it when the olds call me duckie or lovie. In her day, she said, they got a decent price for a decent service, that's just what Mum woulda said. She often said stuff like that, not that she used the bus very much, she liked to walk, saying that's what God gave us legs for.

Mum was really fit, even at the end. She's dead now, died of a stroke. It was terrible at the time, a total shocker, but we just have to pick ourselves up and push our way through it, I s'pose.

Mum was always good at cheering me up too. No matter how bad it got, and let's face it, bad is my middle name. If I ever had a crap day at school or anything she'd say, "Now Nessa, don't take on so. We all can't be good at everything, you don't have to be Einstein for God to love you, or me neither." Then she'd pop a kiss on the top of my head, I used to love that – made me feel that everything was all right. But she was a one, she used to love a drink. Like daughter like mother, that's how the saying goes, innit? Never stopped giving me a laugh – I'd come home late from the club and there she'd be, lying on the sofa catching flies, her mouth and legs wide open. Funny how easy I can see her in my head just when I want to, as if she were right smack bang in front of me.

When my Cherry was born I was made up. I'd never done anything I'd been really proud of before, and Mum, well, she was just over the moon. But she never approved when I first fell, me not being married and all. "You can get more than wet knickers from a fumble up a back alley." Not sure what he was even called. Mum went crazy for a bit, it went against her religious beliefs and that. But she never gave up on me and at last she said, "It's not for me to judge, we'll leave that to the good Lord in heaven. It is my job to love." She wasn't married though, just took Dad's name. Sneaky fucking cow, never said. Only found out when she died. Dad was already married, couldn't get a divorce. They were sinners; they've been forgiven though and moved on. Not like me.

I really miss Mum, but as she'd say, she's in God's hands now so no need to get all sorry for myself. Mum used to dote on Cherry. Spoilt her rotten. That time, I'll never forget it, Cherry must have been about a year, she was in a buggy anyway, and that Glynnis from number eighty-four said Cherry was a bastard, and that she'd end up just like her mother. Well, Mum went off on one, she knocked her down, right there in the street, smacked her one on the nose. The look on that woman's face was a picture. Served her right for sticking her beak in. Mum wouldn't let something like that go. She was a piece of work. It was hard on Cherry, what with me working shifts. Mum took care of her mainly, tucking her into bed and reading her stories. Cherry didn't much like all her new daddies either.

Are you listening? Don't look like it, cheeky bugger. I can't read on the bus, it makes me feel sick, and the newspaper's full of all that terrible stuff anyhow. Someone's always died or there's been a disaster or some pervert interfering with kids. Makes me puke. Don't know how you can stand it.

I know Mum can hear me. She doesn't blame me, even after all I done. Still gives me advice, telling me to keep my chin up. It was awful those few months that I was sent away and couldn't see her. Mum didn't come to visit me in prison. She said it weighed on her heart to see me there. And I had no one to talk to inside. They were all too busy with their own business. One of them said, "you'd better get it together, you sink or swim in here." Sank like a stone, I did. That's a look-and-a-half, darling. I'm not ashamed to admit I've been inside – I had to pay my dues. That woman's face 'll never look the same again.

You've seen me up at the cemetery before, have you? Well, I'm there every day, regular as clockwork. Can't seem to keep away. I don't remember seeing you. But I should have, you being on the large side and all those gold rings, you're not exactly easy to miss. Sorry love, I'm such a bitch, you're probably happy in your own skin ... That's sad, both your mum and dad gone in a few weeks of one another. It ain't fair them both being so young, not even seventy ... You get lonely – tell me about it. I know where you mean, right up at the back of the cemetery, under the trees. It's lovely there, darlin', I'm sure your parents are happy there.

Goldie, that's what I'll call you, you don't mind, do you, love? I ain't surprised I didn't know you, I'm always in a world of my own. They let me out for mum's funeral. I'd have been heartbroken if not. I didn't mind there weren't many people, I just wanted us all to be together again and that's what mattered, being together – I'm glad they're not alone. Funny, I can remember being released, but not much after that. Went a bit doolally without Mum. And I had to look after my Cherry all by myself. Which was no walk in the park, I tell ya. I've had a terrible sore throat since, can't seem to shake it. That red mark around my neck? I s'pose it might have something to do with it, I've never thought about it. And don't you 'alf wheeze something awful. I'd lay off the ciggies if I were you or you'll end up joining your mum and dad sooner than you thought. Sorry, I know it ain't funny.

Ring the bell, then. It reminds me of that song – *You can ring my bell*, I have to sing it to myself because I'm forever overshooting. Mum was right, she always said "Nessa, if you didn't have your head screwed on, you'd end up draggin' it behind you on a piece of string." And I don't fancy having to walk back in this weather. I don't 'alf feel like a toddler tottering around in my high heels. You don't mind if I grab onto your arm do you, Goldie, or I'll end up arse over tit and crawling off the bus.

I love the sound of the snow crunching under my feet. It's beautiful, the way it sparkles. I remember how I'd nag Dad to go out and play in the snow when

I was a kid. Nagging to go out, and nagging to come back in when I'd had enough – "Dad, I'm cold. My legs hurt." He used to sweep me up, laughing, and carry me home. He was so warm. When Dad died we'd go to the cemetery loads, Mum would bring me to visit his grave and we could spend hours going up and down the rows. Looking at the names and ages on the stones, she'd make up lives for the people underneath them. She loved being shocked when she came across a young man who'd been killed in one of them world wars at only eighteen or nineteen, and disappointed when he was as old as twenty-nine or thirty. Morbid cow.

There you are then, that's my dad, *James Osborne 1945–1989 – Beloved husband and devoted father*, and my mum, *Maureen Osborne 1947–2006 – Much missed mother and grandmother*. Lovely words, ain't they. And here's my beautiful baby – *Cherry Osborne 2000–2007.*

I can't tell you how much I wish she was still with me, that I hadn't left her alone that night and gone out on the lash, but I'm glad that Jesus has Cherry safe as one of his sunbeams. And then this one, *Vanessa Osborne 1982–2007 – May she find peace with God.* You know Goldie, I haven't found any peace yet, I don't deserve it, but one day I'll get to rest with my Cherry.

SURFACE TENSION

Since pressing the send button the previous night, she'd had plenty of time to repent. Modern technology was too convenient; communicating without critical assessment. He'd never be interested in her; she'd been an idiot to think otherwise. And this train was being hopelessly slow. It was already 6.38 and it still hadn't made its first stop. Not today, not today, not today, the train *couldn't* be late, not today. The 6.12 would have been safer, getting her to the office an entire hour before usual. That email must be deleted. He could never see it. Don't ask questions you're afraid to hear the answers to, was advice she'd often given to angst-fuelled friends. It wasn't until she'd sent her declaration that she realised she really didn't want to know the truth. Life was fine, if not perfect, and now she'd jeopardised it.

At least she'd got a double seat to herself. Sirena felt uneasy at being exposed in the larger seating area of the train and this morning she needed to feel protected. She usually enjoyed her commute, savouring its symmetry, going back and forth, as predictable as the tide.

From her safe vantage point, shielded by the high backs of the plastic seats, she observed the carriage. Two young women sat in her direct eye-line, the flesh of their thighs more prominent than their skirts. The blonde nearest to the window spoke as she arranged her long hair in the reflection of the rain-streaked glass.

"He had six shots lined up on the bar. And you know what I'm like on Tequila." The girls both cackled with relish.

Sirena would never let anyone see her drunk and out of control – her humiliation was private. Continuing to crawl, the train had yet to reach any momentum, and she began to panic. Please hurry, please hurry, please hurry.

She thought her own humiliation was in the past. On two notable occasions she'd opened herself to the point of vulnerability. During a school excursion, she'd shared banter with a boy from another class. Throughout the next term she smiled, shouted comments and jokes, and administered playful punches on the boy's arm as he passed in the crowded corridor. Listening to popular love songs, she dreamed of the moment he would ask her to the cinema and at the end of an enchanting evening he would overwhelm her with gentle, tentative kisses. It was when he stopped and asked her, "are you the girl from the field trip?" that she realised he hadn't any clear memory of her. Her adolescent fantasy of soft kisses made her cringe. Later at university, after quashing her nerves, she agreed to a date with a handsome chap from the business school. Surprising herself, she went to his flat with him that evening. Surprise turned to shock when she found herself surrounded by Playboy bunny wallpaper he and his father had put up – as a joke, he assured her. Herself now the rabbit in the headlights, she realised it was far too late to escape. She recalled with a shudder how she'd pushed on his hips, suspending him between her legs, to keep him away. And he was gentlemanly enough to understand. The remainder of the academic year was spent diving into alcoves and behind columns at the sight of any boy with dark hair and olive skin. Finally, the experience was rounded off when the 'trendy' girls asked her to confirm, with obvious disbelief, if she was really 'seeing Dave'.

Given her abject inability to understand men, it seemed sensible to abandon relationships and concentrate on building a career. Until now.

Body heat steamed up the interior of the train carriage. Sirena wiped at the moisture on the window, only managing to make lines of water across the surface. She ran her fingers through the rivulets, creating streams, watching the water pool at the window's frame. At least she was good at her work. She hadn't found it as rewarding as she had expected, and it took a while to adjust her ambitions downward to being an assistant. It wasn't all she'd hoped her career would be, but it suited her. She was in control. It paid well, her colleagues were good company, and despite her position of responsibility, the holidays were flexible. She had no intention of losing it. On the window rain meandered, slow then quick, making its way to the bottom of the glass.

Self-soothing, she reasoned with her anxiety. There was really no need for concern. She was always the first to arrive at work, even though she didn't consider 7.30 to be particularly early. No one on her floor arrived before 8.30. Except for him. She'd been his personal assistant for seven years and he, without exception, arrived at 8am and worked until 9 or 10 at night. She, an early bird, the morning lark, and he a night owl. In reality, there was only an hour between their routines. She never left him much before 8pm.

"Off early again, Sirena?" he'd call to her when she asked him if he needed anything more from her before she packed up for the day.

"Be here all the earlier tomorrow." He'd laugh, satisfied by his own wit and knowing literary reference. Dickens was one of his favourites, but Sirena could never accuse him of Scrooge-like behaviour and his childlike humour amused her.

It was inevitable they would become close: working long hours with one person, not just anyone, but someone she respected and who was always so thoughtful. Even when they were working to a tight deadline, he never made unreasonable or last minute demands of her. He was made all the more appealing by his gentle delivery and relaxed manner. On numerous occasions, he'd made it known that he'd never manage without her, and had not once forgotten her birthday. She cherished the personal message of appreciation he'd send with her present. Occasionally, the way he looked at her, holding her gaze a beat too long, made the possibility of intimate relations real. When he got divorced, he'd confided in her, opening a small window onto his sadness. He admitted he had been lonely for some time, and took her out for a drink. It had raised her hopes for many more social evenings ahead.

But she'd been unable to turn off her professional veneer, uncomfortable at showing any side of herself that was less than the efficient, problem-solving PA they were both used to. She'd organised the table and ordered the drinks, but when it came to cosy chat all that she'd been capable of was practical advice about living alone. He had talked with short, faltering sentences, falling mute, and she'd saved him by reassuring him that being single had its benefits. Competent, helpful and knowledgable. Even on a date she was professionalism personified. Laughing, he'd joked she was much more efficient than a wife.

Then last night, he'd sent the email. Would she go on a business weekend away with him. Her imagination resurfaced, conjuring scenes of hand-holding while walking slowly through an Italian style garden and sharing adoring, but coy, looks across a candlelit table for two. As she reread the email for the umpteenth time, two glasses of red wine endorsed her amorous declaration.

Dear Lord, if only she could unsend it. That would teach her to drink alone.

The train was slowing down, readying itself to stop. It juddered as it halted at the station. The doors parted and people gushed into the carriage, jostling those getting off to step onto the platform. They were sodden and limp, macs and umbrellas dripping and heavy with rain. The doors beeped and slammed shut, locking them in. The smell of sweat and stale alcohol combined and permeated the carriage as the commuters shuffled, vying for position in the narrow gangway. Overwhelmed by the weight of the full carriage, Sirena felt as if she'd been confined in a diving bell and lowered to the extreme depths of the ocean. Her position of safety now felt too enclosed. She was trapped. A woman sat next to her filling the seat, her perfect knees contacting with the chair in front of her. It was as if she could fill any space, however large or small. In contrast to the humid air of the carriage, she was fresh, almost cold. Sirena couldn't look, keeping her head straight ahead but was desperate to turn to the giant shifting and resting next to her. Her mind arrested, locking onto her neighbour.

Before I came to the surface, I didn't realise humans couldn't live under water

But the waves are terrifying and destructive in a storm ...

My sisters and I watched as sailors struggled to save themselves and we sang songs of courage to tell them the sea could be their home

Sirena was confused. She'd been aware of the words, but had heard nothing. She glanced up at the faces of other commuters – they showed no sign of having heard it.

"Can you move down, please?" A woman wearing a green mac shouted into the carriage.

"If you tell me where I can move to then I'd gladly go." The man looked to other passengers to gain support. All eyes lowered to the floor. Half a dozen people shuffled with leaden feet, pushing against one another, a few steps further down into the narrow gangway of the carriage.

"Ladies and gentlemen, I'm sorry but we're being asked to hold at a red light," a voice announced from somewhere unseen in the roof. The carriage exhaled, tired frustration mingled with a touch of resignation. The driver continued, "I'm not sure how long we'll be held here, but I'll let you know when I know."

Sirena clenched her teeth, setting off a wave of tension throughout her body. Please move, please move, please move. The air came and went, bringing oxygen and stealing it away just before she had inhaled enough to satisfy. Her sight dimmed, clarity blurring, speckles destroying shape. Greenblue reflections rippled across the roof of the carriage. Her reptilian eyes followed its quick movement, chasing explanations for her diminished state. The need to swim from the depths to the surface engulfed her.

I bring the sea to shore because I can no longer return

Sirena broke her head away. Rain continued to drizzle, as each drop hit the glass it raced in competition with the others swimming downwards. The voice continued:

Once I saved a drowning man and brought him safe to shore

I loved him, but as I was I could not live on the land

For his love I sacrificed my family, my home and the sea

He did not return my love, but I learned to thrive on land

Through the haze of steam and rain she sees a reflection, lasting only the time it takes to shift the line of vision from one side of the room to another. A cave, where the sea is clear and pure blue beneath the surface tension. Light, rare but determined, reflects off the water to the uneven dome and walls, causing bright shapes to lurch and mutate, illuminating the darkest depressions. Spray forces itself against rock and rebounds, leaping into the air, glowing and luminous as the light passes through it.

You're drowning ...

But you can save yourself: you can reach the surface ...

Swim. Swim up through the waves ...

She's immersed in the sea. Breathing water in, gasping, her small, slim arms uncoordinated, moving in all directions, pushing her down under the waves. The currents take her wherever their whim dictates. Confused, panicked, she thrashes, her head thrusts above the surface – she hears shouting on the beach. The voices abate her panic. Relaxing her chaotic arms, she brings them to order, remembering her lessons and the strokes she has been taught. She is at the surface, breathing, gasping a little as a wave breaks next to her but she is moving forward. Swimming.

Remember what the sea means to you

She's standing on the rock as the waves hit her feet

and cold drops strike her face. Not allowing fear to stop her, she's standing on the edge of a cliff overlooking a rough sea on a rainy day, struggling with the hood of her coat. Nothing stops her getting to the sea. It gives her strength and vitality and makes her feel that she is capable of anything.

The sudden remembrance of her past calls up sight, sound, smell. The thrill of approaching the coast as the sky changes, somehow becoming larger, wider, and the sound of the gulls crying, promising the sea's unseen presence. The coolness of the sand as she buries her feet and watches as her new baby sister, blonde and alert, gnaws at a packet of biscuits topped with sand. Then how she feels when she sees a couple kissing on the beach, screwing up her nose with embarrassment, curious but feigning disgust when her aunt says one day she'll understand.

And she does understand – to expect disappointment and isolation.

Exhilaration gives way to desperation as she realises she is trying to claw her way back to a time before she'd kissed a man. Her life has become so small. Avoiding pleasure or discomfort, satisfied with her routine. Treading water instead of diving into the waves, into life, and swimming through her fears. At some undefined point she stopped wanting to be the one who acted and became the one who followed.

Daring to strain her peripheral vision, she sees the perfect knee flash greenbluesilver, small scales layered smooth on top of one another, the light passing over them, making them shine and glitter like a discoball. Aqua spots shimmer across her face, above her head, then disappear.

Fear will give you Fight

Fight will give you Freedom

Dive in and Swim

"Sorry for the long delay. A train has broken down in front of us. It might be a while yet. I'll let you know when we're ready to move." The driver really did sound sorry.

"Gosh, how inconvenient, I've an important meeting this morning." Stunned by the voice of the woman next to her, Sirena jolted her head to look at her. The woman rummaged in her bag, her face obscured, attentive to her task. Her movements were quick and graceful, counterintuitive to her solid frame. She was well groomed, her short dark hair as sleek as an otter's. As she fished her phone out of her bag, she continued talking to Sirena, her voice deep and soothing, betraying no urgency.

"I'd better let the office know." She was smiling. "How about you? You seem a little anxious." Her fingers moved across the surface of her phone.

With her eyes narrowed and brows pinched, Sirena continued scanning the woman. Receiving silence, the woman looked at Sirena. Sirena couldn't tell if the woman's eyes were green, blue or violet; they seemed to be neither or all but they were bright, even brilliant. Sirena faltered for a moment. She was scared but looking into the woman's eyes lent excitement to her fear. Battling to bring her feelings to order, she remembered how to surge forward. She fought free, no longer hesitant. The need to live forced her up for air. Forced her to break the surface tension and swim.

"Oh no, nothing urgent. I'll deal with it when I get there." Sirena grinned.

Sirena realised she did want to know if he had feelings for her. She didn't know how she'd deal with it, whatever his reaction, but she was sure either way she'd work it out. The woman kept smiling, turned back to her phone and pressed send.

"Done." She put her phone back into her bag and

took a business card from a slender mother-of-pearl case. She passed it to Sirena. Sirena blinked away the moisture from her eyes and read the card. *Mermaid Life Coaching – Challenging the Current.*

The card shone greenbluesilver. Sirena smiled. She could do with a little help to work out what was next. It'd been a while since she'd felt excited about the future and there was no need to hesitate.

BRUISED

A body wasn't found, and after seventy-two hours the search was called off. The coastguard said he'd most likely been taken by the currents and washed out to sea. Esther was stunned. She understood what was happening, but couldn't believe this wasn't another attention-seeking antic. It hadn't been unusual for him to disappear, to return days later making some feeble excuse about a forgotten family event and a dead mobile phone. With Rufus, she could never be sure of anything.

*****

The moon was huge and red. Hovering over the dark earth, as if anticipating a kiss, it followed, keeping them company by the side of the road. Light from the headlamps stretched out in front of the car, illuminating the black road and reflecting brightly as the shining diamonds of cats' eyes. They'd been driving for most of the afternoon.

"Do you have to drive so slowly? It's pathetic." Rufus crossed his arms.

"Please Rufus, I'm doing my best and you can't even drive." Esther wouldn't look at him.

"I'm not a politician either, but it doesn't mean I don't have an opinion." Esther didn't reply, knowing to argue any further was pointless. Rufus kept pushing. "Well I'm just giving my opinion, if you can't handle it maybe you shouldn't drive." He pursed his lips.

"We're only here to meet your friends. It's not my fault the roads are so narrow. And it *is* the middle of winter."

"No one forced you, I could have got a lift on my own." Rufus turned to look out of the window. The size of the moon made Esther uneasy. Running along the sides of the road were slender canals. Ensuring the steering wheel was straight, she kept her arms outstretched until they ached.

It was a relief when they arrived at the village. Silhouettes of the unlit buildings sat hollow and imposing. A church dominated the cluster of cottages clinging to the outer edge of the village green, its spire reaching high into the sky and surrounded by stars, which blinked as if trying to eradicate the residue of sleep. Only the pub welcomed them with glowing windows.

"So where's the beach?" Rufus asked.

"I don't know. I've never been here before." Turning the corner the moon reappeared, its shape deformed and cut by the outlines of fishermen's huts.

Holding onto her bag in one hand, two sleeping bags in the other, and a roll up sponge mattress under her arm, she struggled into the wind; it pushed at her as if warning her to go no further. Rufus had already run ahead to meet his friends.

"Good to see you, Rufus. Now we can get on with the party. What took you so long, everyone's waiting." Beth scolded in their general direction with a friendly tone. Esther was quite sure they weren't waiting for her. She dragged herself through the door and dropped the things on the floor. The hut was freezing, and the air damp. Everyone wore their coats.

"Welcome Esther, I'm afraid we're having to drink neat vodka to keep warm." Beth approached her with a full shot glass. After the handing over ceremony, she was air kissed on both cheeks.

"I'm sure that won't be too much of a task for Rufus. He's already onto his second," Beth said. Everyone laughed – except for Esther. Rufus frowned. He purposely kissed her and mumbled, "Keep your mouth shut, don't embarrass me."

The room was barely furnished, dominated by a large dining table placed in the middle, a well-used kitchenette behind it. In the corner, and to the left of the entrance, was an old TV set on which a man was pleading for his life. He burned, trapped inside an enormous wicker man. In front of the TV was a small wooden framed two-seater sofa, the cushions covered with orange velour. Deborah sat on it with her legs draped across Marc's. A makeshift mermaid, her long floral skirt emerged from the bottom of her coat in a tube, as if a replacement for legs. She leant backwards and held her hand towards Rufus. Her long hair touched the floor, merging with the chocolate swirls of carpet. He slipped his fingers between hers.

"Where are we sleeping?" Esther asked.

"I'll show you." Beth moved to the only other door in the room, opposite the entrance. Esther picked up her bag and one of the sleeping bags.

"Can you help me please, Rufus?" Esther asked. He forced a laugh, released Deborah, and then jogged over to her attempting to show interest. "I want to see where we're sleeping too, you know."

The rest of the building was a maze of small wooden staircases and tiny cabin sized rooms. Their footsteps resonated throughout the structure as they climbed the stairs to their second floor room. It contained nothing, only a bare bulb hung from the centre of the ceiling.

"I'll leave you to it." Beth closed the door behind her, shutting them in. Wind beat against the side of the hut making the glass shudder. Rufus embraced her, sliding his arms low to the base of her back. He kissed her lightly on the lips, looked her in the eye, and smiled.

"We'll have to stay very close tonight to keep warm." She submitted to him, grateful for a respite from his antagonism. He kissed her slowly, working his tongue into her mouth. She could feel the first signs of his arousal. Someone ran up the stairs, the hut shook. He pulled back from her as if she had scalded him.

Six of them sat around the table, eating a rudimentary meal of instant noodles swimming in a thin sauce of tomato and basil.

"It's not exactly Michelin star darling, but I'm sure we'll cope." Paul raised his glass at Beth in an ironic salute.

"You can make your own tomorrow, dear. Have you seen the facilities?" Beth replied. They laughed.

"Well, don't expect me to do any cooking." Deborah rested her elbow on the table, her wine glass dangling by the tips of her fingers. "Drinking is more my speciality." She grinned and gulped at her wine.

"You're not the only one." Paul directed his gaze to Rufus.

"It's the only way I can numb the pain." Esther watched him as he stood up from the table and grabbed at an unopened bottle of red on the only surface of the kitchenette. He was already drunk. "And I need a lot. Anyone else?" Playing the troubled genius drowning his sorrows suited his crowd very well.

Deborah held up her glass and professed, "kindred spirits." Rufus poured her a full glass.

"Has anyone read the latest Kurkarni? The reviews were fantastic," interjected Beth.

Paul always read the reviews. Marc had read Kurkarni's previous book and would definitely be looking into it – he was a wonderful writer with such refreshing ideas. All of Rufus's friends were artistic or creative in some way; their lives revolved around reading literature and attending cultural events. Beth was a fabulous artist who already had exhibitions. This was the kind of group Esther had longed to be part of when growing up, but now that she was, she just felt inadequate. It was as if she had a cultural deficiency, and the time and energy she invested in reading never took it from the red to the black. However, Rufus often said she would be the only one at the table to have actually read a book, but the only one to also keep quiet about it. She could never find the words. When she spoke, her voice was too quiet to hold people's attention. It infuriated him.

"Esther's read Kurkarni." Rufus stared at her, forcing her to join the conversation.

"Really? Any good?" Marc scrutinised her over the top of his glasses.

"I'm not keen on the way he describes women's breasts: they're always small, but pert," Esther offered. Beth laughed aloud.

"Yes, you're right, they are – I'd never thought of that before." Esther was permitted to be quiet again.

"Happy New Year!"

Being the only place in the village open, the pub was packed. Esther was squashed amongst groups of friends as they greeted the New Year. Arms struggled free, and glasses clinked in the air. Then came *Auld Lang Syne*, at first strong and clear, but soon mumbled and indistinct. Rufus lunged from the other side of the group, pushing forward to kiss her. Grabbing her around the waist, he forced his lips hard onto hers. It hurt. He dropped her, turning to take a drink offered to him by Deborah.

"Let's go down to the beach." Beth was excited.

"But it's freezing." Rufus pushed his lips together into a pout.

"Come on, don't be a baby." Deborah thrust her arm though his, forcing him through the crowd, towards the door. The others followed. Rufus, Deborah and Marc marched ahead, disappearing into the dark. Paul and Beth walked slightly in front of Esther, holding hands. Beth turned back to Esther.

"You okay?"

Esther smiled and nodded.

"This is certainly the weather to make your bosoms pert," Esther said. Beth laughed again.

"You know Esther, I didn't get what Rufus saw in you at first, but now I get it." Esther was confused at whether this was a compliment. In response, she clasped both hands to her breasts.

"Is it my pert bosom?" They both laughed.

Approaching the huts, the sound of the river could be heard. It was disorientating, seemingly coming from all around them. Behind the slender beach huts, a large hump loomed. The glowing moonlight floated above it, blacking out the details of the vegetation running along its top. Esther could hear the shouts belonging to the others far ahead of them. A figure ran up the sand dune, and for a moment a perfect silhouette stood.

"I can smell the sea."

Rufus's voice carried to them, directed by the wind. He ran down the other side and out of sight. Another figure scrabbled to the top and then disappeared. Esther guessed it to be Deborah.

Sand tumbled over Esther's shoes as she scrambled down the bank and onto the beach. The tide was out, making the beach huge. The moon hung low, its dim creamy light gleaming on small pools of water collected in the hardened ribbed sand. As it dispersed, the river lost its shape and was swallowed by the sea. There were laughs and screams coming from dark unidentifiable figures. For the atmosphere of the beach alone, the trip had been worth making.

She knew she ought to at least try to find Rufus. He'd only be angry with her for not keeping up with him if she didn't, but she was happy on the beach by herself. Walking towards the sea she smelt the salty air. It was fresh and clean, and she relaxed, allowing herself to enjoy the freedom of solitude. As she arrived at the water's edge, the wind blew harder and the tide started to turn. It was coming in much quicker than she'd anticipated. A wave broke and the water ran forward, layers overtaking one another until it jumped over her shoes. This was the dangerous part of the coastline. With numerous rivulets running from the land, it was easy to get cut off from the shore without realising it. Esther started to walk fast towards the dunes. She'd didn't bother letting the others know; she would see them back at the hut.

Esther struggled out of her thermal top and into her pyjamas. Dark purple, the bruise lingered, although the edges had started to lighten towards a delicate lavender hue. The teeth marks, which broke the skin, had scabbed over, but it was still sore to the touch. He'd been angry that he couldn't find his passport and had blamed her. It was their first Christmas as a married couple; she was going away with her new husband to prove to herself and her family that she was happy. From Belgium, they had come straight back to join his friends for New Year's Eve. After his anger over the passport, she'd dreaded their Christmas trip to Bruges. At least when he was with his friends the most he did was flirt and sulk and drink. His friends were used to that. Esther pulled a baggy jumper over the pyjama top. She filled a hot water bottle, made a cup of tea, and read until the others got back.

"He ran off – I thought he'd be back before me." Deborah inhaled on her cigarette, exhaling the smoke hard in front of her.

Paul persisted. "But you were the last to see him. Are you sure you can't remember which direction he went?"

"No, you've seen it out there. It's hard to tell, there's so little light, and I just assumed he'd come straight back." She inhaled on her cigarette again, uncomfortable at being questioned. The door opened. Everyone looked up to expect Rufus, but Marc entered alone.

"No sign of him at the pub and the tide's right in. It's come quite far up tonight, only about ten metres from the sand dunes."

"I think we should call the police," Beth said. "I'm getting worried and Esther must be frantic. I would be if it were you." She smiled with concern at Paul and then at Esther.

Esther forced a laugh. "You know what he's like, and he often wanders off on his own. No trace to be found."

"But not on a dark beach with the tide coming in – and him being so drunk. I'm calling the police." Paul dialled his mobile phone.

*****

It was late and she just wanted the train to get going. Her recce was early, and the journey would give her a chance to get some work done; to prepare the best she could and then relax a little before arriving at Bristol. Her phone rang to let her know she had a new message. It was her friend Daisy:

"Let me know how it's going. Can't wait to catch up." The phone beeped and another message played.

"On my way. You'd better be back before me. I've got something for you." Rufus was drunk and his words slurred. Esther pulled the phone from her ear. She felt sick. For a second she re-imagined her life with Rufus; his disappearance just an elaborate trick. The phone beeped again and told her the message was fourteen months old. She didn't remember hearing it before.

Since he had gone, she'd started to salvage her life. At first Esther had grieved, but wasn't sure what for exactly. He was too young. It was a waste of talent. There was a hole left in all their lives. But not for him, not for his own sake, not really. Appalled at her response, she'd felt guilty and confused. His friends had been supportive for a few months, but without Rufus to bind them together the routine of their lives returned, and they disappeared from hers as much as Rufus had.

Sitting back in her seat she closed her eyes. Loud clattering made her open them again. A man was dragging his bike onto the carriage. Continuing to pull it behind him, he dropped in the seat next to her, blocking the exit. She hoped he hadn't done it on purpose to trap her. The carriage was busy, so Esther reassured herself she had nothing to worry about. For a while at least.

"You don't mind if I sit here, do you? I just want to be near my bike." It was a little too late to ask permission, so Esther just smiled and glanced sidelong at him without looking him in the face. He might stay on as far as Bristol. She began to plan her escape.

The man laughed. "No need to worry, I'm not a rapist." He continued laughing. She didn't look at him, embarrassed that he'd read her mind. "Can you believe I turn forty next week?" Esther, still unable to look at him, forced an empty grin. "No need to answer – I probably look ancient to you. You can't be more than twenty-five." He laughed again.

"I wish." She'd surprised herself by answering him. Esther looked at him, allowing herself to smile. "I'm a bit older than that."

Esther liked him. He was funny and direct, but had a kindness to his voice. He told her he worked for the civil service as a policy advisor. She wasn't surprised; his brusque manner suggested he wasn't used to wasting time. Esther explained she was making a film for her latest work project, and she was going to meet some potential interviewees and visit a few locations. He was impressed.

"Gosh, that sounds very complicated. So you don't just point and shoot?"

"Oh no, not really. Sometimes I have to do it on the hoof, but if there's time and money I'll do a recce. It does make the filming easier." Esther was uncomfortable at explaining her work.

"I'm sure your films are always good. Better than mine would be at any rate. I'm hopeless with a camera, I never fail to chop someone's head off." Esther laughed as he bashed his flattened hand into his forehead.

"Thank you, you're very kind to say that, but there's so much to learn." She was pleased he'd been interested, but it was true, she never felt she knew enough or had done her best. Aspects of the shoot she could have improved replayed in her mind for days later. If only she'd been faster or more resourceful.

The train began to slow.

"Next stop Reading: Reading is the next stop."

"Oh well, that's me." He paused for a moment and then continued. "I guess we'll never see each other again."

During the past year she'd met a few men who'd been interested in her, but she wasn't ready to think of another relationship. An automatic thought intruded – you don't meet many people you actually like straight away.

"Why don't you give me your number?" Esther couldn't believe she'd said it aloud. He smiled and held out his hand.

"Alexander Wheeler-Pickles." Esther laughed as they shook hands.

"Wheeler-Pickles? I don't believe you." He pulled his cash card from his wallet and showed her.

"There you are, Wheeler-Pickles." She laughed again. He took out a fountain pen and she watched as he wrote his number on a piece of folded paper. After he finished he stood up, disentangled his bike, and pushed it to the door. Turning around, he gave her a small wave. She waved back.

"Cheerio then. Onwards." He lifted his bike from the train and she watched, smiling as he pushed it along, half-illuminated under the dim lighting of the platform, towards the exit.

You thought I'd gone.

Esther cried out, grabbing her arm. The pain was excruciating, as if someone was biting into her flesh. She sat up and turned on the bedside lamp. A large bruise stained the top of her left arm. Teeth marks ran around the edge in two curved lines, blood seeping from the broken skin.

I've come back for you.

Esther panicked, and ran across the small hotel room in Bristol to check the window. It was closed.

She shouted out as she approached the bathroom.

"Who's there?" Putting her hand inside the door, she pulled on the light cord. The bathroom was empty. She checked the door. It was still locked.

You don't need anyone else.

Seeking the source of the voice she spun her head around. There was nobody there. Returning to the bed she sat on the edge and inspected the bruise again. It was hideous and she was frightened. She remembered the evening Rufus had torn their house apart looking for his passport. He'd pulled the contents of every drawer and every cupboard out onto the floor, searching through the papers and documents with a kind of mania. When they failed to yield the passport, he kicked them across the floor, pages curling as if protecting each other.

"I should have known better than to leave it to you." He'd shouted, his anger increasing until he'd taken hold of her and bit her hard, without constraint, drawing blood.

"This is my own fault for being with someone so pathetic." He'd shoved her away. Esther had stumbled, and held onto a chair, frightened of slipping on the papers. Frightened of him. He'd passed out on the sofa drunk. She'd tiptoed around him, looking for his passport. Making sure not to wake him, she replaced the scattered items into their original places. The passport was hidden amongst paperwork he'd been preparing for his tax return. She placed it on top of his travel bag where he could see it when he awoke. Once everything was tidied away she'd dressed her wound and gone to bed.

Finally, Esther gave up her search for the source of the voice. Instead, she took the piece of paper Alexander had given her out of her bag and looked at the telephone number. His handwriting was beautiful. The numbers were bold and curved into exaggerated digits. She ran her thumb across the paper to make sure they were real.

He can't have you.

She turned around and saw Rufus lounging on the hotel bed, lying on his side with his head propped up by his arm. He inhaled on a cigarette and blew the smoke at her.

Only I can.

*****

"Okay, so you're gonna call him, right? He sounds fab." Esther stared down into her coffee. Daisy continued.

"You have to – you need to move on." Esther hadn't heard from Rufus since his appearance at the Bristol hotel, but the bruise remained. He'd be back. Daisy was the only person she'd shown her bruise to the first time, and her conclusion was final. Get rid of him. Then he had disappeared.

"Daisy, don't think I'm going mad."

Daisy sighed. "What is it now …"

Esther interrupted Daisy. Slipping her arm from her jumper, she showed Daisy the bruise. Daisy looked at Esther's arm.

"What?" She was confused.

"It happened the other night when I was at Bristol."

"What happened? I don't know what you're showing me." Esther could see the deep purple bruise and feel its ache.

"You can't see anything?"

"No. I think you are defo going mad." Esther

put her jumper back on.

Rufus laughed.

She can't help you.

Here he was again, whispering and cajoling. He was right, Daisy couldn't help her. He'd said he had come back for her. She wasn't surprised – Rufus was too spiteful to let her move on.

"Now, about this Alexander. Call him and make a date. I approve wholeheartedly, from what you say he seems like a proper grown-up. And if you don't then I will." Daisy snatched the paper from Esther's hand. Esther picked up her phone. Daisy held the number in front of her and Esther dialled.

You're worthless.

Rufus breathed into her ear. His breath slid down her neck, moving over her body. She placed the phone onto the table, as if it was responsible for weighing down her arms. Esther stared at Daisy.

"I can't do it, Daisy."

"You can. Now, get on with it." Daisy picked it back up.

It's humiliating.

She knew Rufus meant what he said. He would wear her down, contaminate her with his vitriol and draw her back into his toxic world. Esther couldn't stop him in life. She didn't know how it could be done in death.

"For heaven's sake Esther, grow some balls." Daisy started to call the number. It rang.

Shameful.

"No, stop. Daisy, please don't …" She snatched the phone from Daisy's hand and ended the call. Esther could almost feel the weight of his body against her back, pressing his hands down her arms and taking her strength. The bruise hurt as he squeezed her.

"Come on Esther, fix up. We're doing this even if it kills you." Daisy almost shouted it.

Even if it killed her. Rufus might just be capable of it. She had proof he could still hurt her. But Daisy was right. Esther grabbed the sheet of paper. At the bottom was half an email address: alexanderwpickles@gov. The paper was a print-out of an old message, but the address had been cut off.

"Okay, okay, I'll email him. It's a government address, so I can easily work out the other part."

Daisy sat over her while she wrote her message.

21.32 TO BRISTOL TEMPLE MEADS.

Dear Alexander,

I hope you're well.

It was a Brief Encounter, but pleasant nonetheless. Would you like to meet again for a drink, or possibly dinner? Are you free over the next few days?

I've been preparing hard for my Bristol shoot. It would be good to have a break and enjoy a lovely evening out.

Best,

Esther Mitchell

"It's a bit basic, but the joke is a nice touch."
"What else is there to say?"

Only I want you.

"At least put your mobile number." Esther added her number.
"Shall I send it?"
"Yes!"

Only I can have you.

"This is a mistake." Daisy reached over and pressed send.
"I can't believe you just did that."
"Relax. What's the worst that can happen?"

Only I can love you.

"He won't answer, he'll think I'm stupid or needy or desperate."

"No, he'll think you're a beautiful, intelligent woman who is interested in him sexually. He'll be flattered. Who wouldn't be?"

Stupid, needy and desperate.

"Daisy I feel sick."

I'll never let you go.

"Now we wait."

The reply was immediate.

Automatic reply: 21.32 TO BRISTOL TEMPLE MEADS.

I will be out of the office for the rest of the day and will attend to any business on my return.

If your enquiry is urgent, please contact my colleague, Emily Bloom, on: 020 3448 6758.

Regards,

Alexander Wheeler-Pickles

Esther regretted sending the email. An instant rejection would have been hard, but to wait for his reply was excruciating.

*****

It had been hours and she hadn't slept. She could feel him breathing behind her. He was lying close to her back, so close she couldn't move. Esther was trapped on the edge of the bed, staring into the darkness, wide awake. Their shared possessions filled the room, surrounding her. To move may mean he would speak again, and she would do anything to prevent hearing his renewed venom. His words clung to her, creeping around her and containing her, like his cigarette smoke, which saturated her lungs and took her breath. Waking Rufus was like playing a game of Russian roulette. She'd lie next to him, afraid of the moment he'd open his eyes. If he started in a bad mood, he would continue like that for the entire day. Everything she did would be put under scrutiny and criticised, which would build until he would run off to get drunk. He'd threaten her, claiming he'd find someone better to spend the day with. She would pay so she'd better make it right, or else. Negotiating every conversation left her exhausted and bereft.

During the next day, she checked her emails hourly. Every fifteen minutes she stared at her inbox. At 17.46 she received a reply.

21.32 TO BRISTOL TEMPLE MEADS.

Dear Esther,

I am well, and I trust you are too.

It's such a delight to hear from you. You've made my day. To be honest I didn't think you'd be interested in an old bear like myself.

How about next Tuesday? I'm busy settling into a new post at the moment, sorry it can't be sooner. Centre of town is good for me.

Take care now. And good luck with the shoot. I think what you do is fab, you know.

Let me know what suits. Onwards.

Kind Regards,

Alexander Wheeler-Pickles

Her initial excitement was replaced by disappointment. Next Tuesday was an entire week. She couldn't understand – if he wanted to see her why didn't he offer to meet sooner, or at least this weekend. Everybody knows Monday and Tuesday are reserved for low priority social engagements. Esther was confused, unsure how to take it.

You can't be sure.

He was whispering again, breathing hard into her neck. A cold feeling slid down her body, raising her body hair as it moved. She was so tired.

*****

Rufus had been erratic in his behaviour when they'd first started going out. They had met at work, her first creative job since graduating. She'd spent nearly three years working in shops and pubs, and was beginning to think her parents were right: she'd never make a living from art. At last, she'd been taken on as a junior web producer. The role meant she was expected to produce the web content for a high profile arts magazine. She had to write copy, choose pictures, and shoot and edit video. Esther had a boss who oversaw what she did, but the budgets for the web were so low she had to complete most of the work herself. It was a fantastic opportunity and Esther was elated to get it. She was also completely overwhelmed.

Esther was afraid to make suggestions, and under her direction the webzine merely reflected the printed magazine. Her boss was happy with her work as far as it went, but was keen for her to bring some originality and 'edge' to it. 'Edge' had never been her forte. It was Rufus who'd helped her to build her confidence. Being a freelance photographer, he regularly gave her pictures to choose for the cut-down articles.

One morning he'd found her crying after a meeting with her boss. When she'd explained, Rufus had asked her to go to an independent exhibition with him. They had discussed how she could use these types of exhibitions and link them to features in the magazine to give it an interesting dimension. Just talking to him had helped her to formulate a plan and develop her way of looking at her role on the magazine. Rufus was older than her, he was confident and cool; an established photographer who seemed to know everything and everybody. She was flattered by his interest in her. Most of the girls in the office fancied him, and it raised her kudos amongst them to be seen with him.

Soon after she'd been out with him, she was told he'd been seeing someone else in the office. But he'd thrown her over to be with Esther.

She was hooked.

But Rufus was confusing. Attentive and loving one week, yet the following she'd hear nothing from him at all. She spent hours trying to work out what she'd done wrong. Often she imagined what psychological torment kept him away from her, or what creative urges had overtaken him. He and his camera could be shooting anything. On other occasions he'd be cruel, making personal comments about her appearance, her education, and what he saw as her misunderstanding of the world. Wearing the wrong cardigan incited disdain. She was defenceless, and when she asked him what he gained from being so mean, believing her honesty would enable him to be candid, he replied,

"If you have to ask, you're more stupid than I thought."

Through a mutual friend she discovered he had a long-term girlfriend, who lived in a different city. The lack of weekends, and increasingly broken arrangements, then made sense. Devastated, Esther booked a trip abroad to make the break from him. Six weeks later he called her in the middle of the night, drunk and crying, saying he'd made a terrible mistake. He was sorry, and couldn't live without her. He said he'd broken off with the other woman. She believed him.

Esther now understood: lying was something some people did. Like trainspotting, or running marathons.

She hoped Alexander wasn't the same as Rufus, but she couldn't know for sure. He was offering her Tuesday, so she took it.

*****

Esther read on the internet that exorcism could evict spiritual entities from a person, or a place. What took place depended on the religion, but all seemed to involve swearing an oath, performing an elaborate ritual, and commanding the spirit to depart in the name of a higher power. Her parents were Christian, and as a child she had believed to please them. She'd enjoyed the stories and festivals that marked out the year and promised special foods and gifts. Esther passed a C of E church on her way home. She no longer believed in God. But she didn't used to believe in ghosts either.

Since she'd last been to a vicarage things had changed. The house was modern and streamlined, and the vicar was a woman. The sign read 'Rev. A. Baxter'.

"Please sit down. Can I get you anything to drink?" Esther was surprised at the glamorous vicar. Her hair and make-up were perfect, and her clothes were smart. Her appearance was an echo of her immaculate house.

"No, thank you. I'm fine."

Reverend Baxter leant forward, inviting Esther to speak. "What can I do for you?"

"It's hard to know what to say. It's my …"

Reverend Baxter smiled gently. "There's no rush."

Esther took a breath and blurted, "My ex-husband is haunting me."

Reverend Baxter frowned. "I'm sorry to hear that. It's very serious."

Esther was relieved that she believed her.

Reverend Baxter continued, "I strongly recommend you contact the police immediately."

Seeing Esther's reaction, Reverend Baxter stood up, energised by her advice.

Esther was bewildered. "Police?"

"Yes, and you must keep a record of all the times he contacts you, or tries to follow you. It's important to have a complete picture for the police. Keep a diary."

"But *you* don't need to know that, if we are trying to get rid of him."

"I can support you emotionally and spiritually of course, but stalking is a police matter. I can also give you the number for the women's refuge in the community. Our first priority is to keep you safe."

Esther was exasperated. "You don't understand, he's haunting me, following me. I can't get rid of him."

"Haunting is a great way to describe it. I'll just get you the number. We can call Janey at the shelter now, together, if it's too difficult for you alone."

Reverend Baxter smiled as she left the room but she hadn't understood Esther at all. Opposite her sat Rufus, laughing. For once, she wanted to join in.

*****

Her choice of dress was flattering, but an extremely tight fit. Rufus stood next to her, staring into the mirror.

You look like a whore.

It was ridiculous for her to agree to this date. Her stomach churned, and her body felt so weak, to the point she doubted her ability to hold herself up.

Rufus's clothes still hung in the wardrobe. With the uncertainty surrounding his disappearance, Esther had found it hard to know what to do with all of his things. Inaction was her decision.

Wading through her wardrobe for the fourth time, she pulled at various garments. *Too showy, too formal, too short.* She struggled out of the dress, and stepped into the comfort of her jeans. Yet they didn't look right either.

Don't fight me. You always fight. Why not just stop.

Esther sank into her bed in exhaustion. She wouldn't go. This was too much. Her frustration mounted in her throat, and she wanted to sob. As she picked up her phone to cancel, Rufus stroked her hair.

Stay with me. You know I will always love you. Stay with me tonight.

Esther wanted to sleep so she could let her body rest. It would be easier to stay with Rufus. Her phone beeped, and she read the text. It was from Daisy:

Good luck. If you're thinking of wimping out then don't. I want to know all about it ASAP.

She had to go.

Esther stood in the doorway, and searched the room for Alexander. Dark wood panelling covered the walls, brass lamps jutting out at regular intervals. A cluster of colourful diamonds stretched across the floor as light shone through the stained glass windows. It was busy, and groups of people gathered around tables, chatting and laughing.

Esther was a few minutes late, so it gave her an advantage. She didn't want to sit in the pub alone, waiting to be stood up. Possibly she would not recognise Alexander. The only thing she could remember about his appearance was the top of his head. His hair was very dark, but it was fine. The harsh lights in the train magnified the meagre strands barely covering his scalp. But his voice was deep and reassuring, she remembered his precise pronunciation. His tone had an energy and humour to it, which she'd liked as soon as he spoke.

At the far side of the bar she saw him sit down at an empty table. It was a relief – he was much better looking than she'd expected. Although his hair was thinning, he still had lots left. He wore a suit and looked well groomed. Esther felt embarrassed and inadequate in her jeans and casual shirt. She'd made a stupid choice for her first date with a civil servant, as he was bound to be smart.

On looking up, he saw her and grinned. He stood and walked over to kiss her on the cheek.

"Good to see you, you look lovely. Sit down, and I'll get you a drink."

He pulled out the wooden chair and she sat. Looming over her, Alexander was enormous.

"What will it be?"

"Gin and tonic, please."

"Righty-ho. I'll be back in a minute."

Righty-ho, Onwards, and *Cheerio.* His bygone mode of speech was charming – the exact opposite of Rufus and his 'arty' group of friends.

Watching him make his way to her, drinks in hand, she knew it was too late to back out. Esther smiled her thanks, and Alexander said something she couldn't hear. She leant forward, fixing her gaze on his lips, willing herself to hear him. She saw his lips move and heard the sounds, but struggled to find meaning to his verbal flow.

Rufus leant in close beside her, his stale breath invading her space.

Vacuous and empty-headed.

She couldn't speak.

Time passed and she sat mute, unable to offer anything to the conversation. Alexander talked regardless, filling the space between them with his experiences of social faux-pas and misdemeanours. He informed her about his disastrous blind date with a police officer. Being nervous he'd got drunk beforehand and spent the entire date demonstrating his *Columbo* impression by repeating, '*Just one more thing.*'

"As you can imagine, Esther, there was no second date. Another drink?"

Esther was so grateful. She laughed at everything he said a little too much. She leant a little too close, and gazed at him a little too fixedly. The pressure to speak was mounting. Even the most sympathetic person would find it hard to sustain a one-sided conversation all evening.

Insipid and tedious.

She could think of nothing to say, her grin awkward between swigs of her drink.

She decided to start with her family. Her family was large and they got on well – most of the time. She could talk about her parents. It was a safe subject, and something she would get right.

Your mother got fucked for a living.

Hobbies and interests: she'd forgotten everything she'd ever liked. Except for Blur, and that was only because she wore a badge to remind her of it.

You've got the taste of a prepubescent girl.

"Shut up, shut up. Leave me alone." Esther stood up as if she were arguing with someone.

"Who are you talking to? You can sit down, you know."

He'd think she was mad now.

"No one. I'm okay, I'm just thinking aloud, thanks."

I'll never leave you alone.

"No need to look so worried." Alexander smiled at her as she sat back down.

Rufus couldn't win. Esther had to think of something to say.

"We'd never have met normally."

She gulped at her drink.

"No, you being a creative type, and me a government drone. It was meant to be."

"Like a cheesy novel." It was like a scene from terrible romance fiction. She cringed, but Alexander didn't seem to mind.

"I think what you do is awfully interesting, Esther."

Esther looked into her drink for reassurance.

"Thank you, but it is hard work." She didn't want to sound arrogant.

He watched her, listening.

"But you enjoy it?" he asked.

"Yes, I do, and I want to be good at it. You can't show fear at all. You have to look like you know what you're doing all the time. I'm terrified, and spend most of my time pretending, or adopting a stiff upper lip." She stiffened her upper lip to demonstrate, and they laughed.

"Sounds a lot like politics really, except politics isn't as interesting," Alexander continued, laughing.

"I can't imagine you being scared, and, besides, you get to help people."

Alexander guffawed, and his laughter made her feel naïve and flustered.

"That's the theory anyway," he replied.

Alexander explained how he had rented a flat near St James' Park for years, but his landlord had wanted the property back at short notice. A friend living in Reading had offered him temporary accommodation. He hated the commute, but he'd endure it for a short time until he found a place closer to the city. She told him she lived alone in her North London house.

"I thought I'd find living on my own tough, but I like looking after myself, like a real grown-up." She didn't tell him it had given her the opportunity to get over her fear of being alone.

It was too late to go for a meal and Alexander had to get to Paddington to catch his train.

"Sorry to cut it short, I'm so busy at the moment. I've got to keep my head."

He pushed his bike alongside her as he walked Esther towards the tube station.

Esther was silent again. Moving from the pub to the street had taken away her temporary confidence. They stopped at the entrance to the tube station and she stood staring at him. He leant in to kiss her on the cheek, but expecting a full kiss, Esther opened her mouth wide, misjudged the manoeuvre and offered a gaping chasm. He drew back and laughed.

"I admire your enthusiasm, but shall we try that again." He didn't give her time to withdraw, and kissed her.

Inane and inadequate.

She could feel Rufus breathing onto her neck.

"That's better. Hopefully, I'll see you soon." Alexander mounted his bike.

She watched him cycle along the road, disappearing into the traffic.

You can't even get him to fuck you.

She agreed with Rufus. 'Disaster' was the word that best summed up the evening. It had been a failure. Each recollection of any aspect of the date stung her with a renewed humiliation. Her silence, the constant idiotic smiling, and her pointing out their meeting was like a cheesy novel. He'd think she was into that kind of chick-lit, how embarrassing. The nadir had to be her gaping cake-hole of a kiss. Awful. Esther was sure she'd never hear from him again and she couldn't blame him. Esther wouldn't want to see herself either.

*****

Esther struggled out of her shirt. The bruise was deep in colour, very much as it had been when it first appeared, the wound still fresh.

You'll always be tainted.

These words mingled with the rancid stench of booze and cigarettes. Moving through the house the smell stalked her, lingering as if Rufus had walked through each room just before her. She sat on her bed and checked her phone. If Alexander had left her a message it might mean he wasn't put off completely. But there was nothing. She wouldn't contact him – it would just cause more humiliation. If he didn't contact her again, she had lost no more face. It wouldn't matter if she slipped away into oblivion.

Her visit to Reverend Baxter a failure, she had to find someone else to help her. She opened her laptop and typed 'How to get rid of a ghost' into the search engine. Various articles popped up. One entitled 'Why People Believe in Ghosts' drew her attention. It outlined a theory regarding the way the brain processes external agents. The article used human evolution as an explanation, suggesting that humans are predisposed to be overly sensitive towards predators, or prey. Once upon a time, this was a life skill, where the fortunate ones who mastered this ability could live to reproduce. Surviving meant even hearing a rustle in the bushes as a potential threat. Human instinct is to spin round, to look for a sinister agent. But there's no one there – just the wind in the leaves. So Rufus was a figment of her oversensitivity towards a predator. Psychology has an explanation for everything, except how to rid oneself of haunting figments.

It was easy for Esther to make a resolution not to contact Alexander, but she found the reality of keeping it unbearable. To protect herself from disappointment, Esther attempted to work hard. She was desperate to distract herself from her growing sense of inadequacy. Her ability to concentrate diminished, she checked her phone or email constantly. She looked Alexander up on various websites, which directed her to a government page. Only his name and basic details of his job description were listed. He didn't appear on any social media sites.

Esther couldn't concentrate for more than a few minutes. Often she escaped to make some tea, or checked something with a colleague. Her days were being wasted.

Sitting in the cinema alone, she felt adrift. Watching a film had given her respite, and also a legitimate reason to turn her phone off for a few hours. Unable to move, Esther watched the end credits of the film roll up in front of her. She took out her phone and turned it on. No messages. She could ring him, but it had only been three days. There was a rule about not calling too early after a date. He might be waiting for the appropriate time. Esther knew this to be nonsense; he just didn't seem to be the type of man to be concerned about frivolous made up dating rules. If he wanted to speak to her, he would.

The next morning she decided it would be reasonable to send an email, letting him know she had enjoyed his company. There could be nothing wrong in that. He could then take the lead on a second date. She spent forty minutes finding the appropriate words.

THANK YOU

Dear Alexander,

I hope you and your bike are well, and that commuting isn't too demanding.

Thank you for a pleasant evening on Tuesday and for being so kind. Hopefully, we will get around to eating next time.

And I'll do some talking too – if you're lucky.

Best,

Esther Mitchell

After it was sent, she knew the email was a mistake. She was sick at chasing a man who clearly wasn't interested. Prompting him would make no difference, and would just make her look foolish. Her stupid joke about talking made her want to hide under her desk. Her email rebounded with the same automated 'Out of Office' message. She felt stupid. The message hadn't said he would be out of the office longer than a day. He might email tomorrow.

She received nothing the next day. Esther had to know if she had really made a mess of it, but dreaded the certainty of his rejection. She decided to ring him when she got home. Making herself comfortable, she dialled his number. Her heart was beating so fast she thought she would have an attack. His phone was switched off.

"Errm, Alexander, it's Esther Mitchell. Just wanted to say hello, so 'Hello.'" She sang the word. "And to tell you I had a nice time the other night, I hope you did too." She was shaking and her mouth was dry.

When my phone was turned off …

She tried again an hour later but it was still off. This

time she didn't bother with a message.

I couldn't be bothered to speak with you ...

Esther knew how deluded she seemed to keep trying, but couldn't stop.

... or I was fucking someone else.

Throughout the evening she stared at her phone. Esther picked it up, put it down, sent numerous unimportant text messages, and turned it on and off. Then she listened to her answerphone, to see if Alexander had left a message while her phone was off. Holding her phone in her hand, she fell asleep on the sofa.

Esther received an email from Alexander the following week.

HELLO

Dear Esther,

I received your message and email. I apologise for my delayed reply, I've been camping with a friend. It was a jolly pleasant trip, good weather.

How about we meet for a meal next Wednesday?

You have a sweet telephone voice.

Let me know if this suits you. Onwards.

Kind Regards,

Alexander Wheeler-Pickles

She couldn't understand why he hadn't mentioned the camping trip. It was a breach of trust, and impossible to form a relationship if he didn't tell her things.

He'll never let you in.

She felt rejected. Why he used 'Kind Regards' she didn't know. They should be beyond such formalities by now. Besides, their meeting would be delayed another week. Again. Esther was too sad to answer straight away. It was making her feel so unhappy, but she liked him and he was funny. He'd been so patient on the date, when she'd been so pathetic.

Esther flicked on the kettle to boil. Her teapot had been a wedding gift, and was a beautiful object. She enjoyed pouring the tea, watching the perfect stream of golden fluid fill the cup. The pot reminded her of her wedding. It had been a beautiful day, and it had gone according to plan. Except for Rufus.

From the moment they were married he'd left her side and ran around from person to person, grabbing at his forelock and laughing: "I can't believe I've done this."

Esther had followed behind, watching as he lit a cigarette outside of the registry office, laughing with his friends. She smiled at her guests as they congratulated and embraced her. Her parents told her they were proud of her and that they'd been wrong not to support her through art college. Rufus was proof that art could be a successful profession and they respected him.

Rufus was drunk, and when they were alone in the taxi on the way to their hotel, he took the opportunity to let her know his true opinion of the day.

"What on earth are you wearing? You look absurd."

He was becoming angry. Later that night, instead of making love he'd shouted at her.

"What was that reception all about? You've always been cheap."

Esther stared at him as he shouted. Her triumph at marrying a man who said he'd never commit evaporated. He just kept shouting and shouting, and wouldn't stop. She had made him this mad. After years of trying to prove to her parents she could be a success, they had admitted they were wrong. It felt amazing. To ruin their relationship again, after all the conflict between them, was unthinkable. She could never admit she'd made a mistake. Esther had created her own prison.

You'll never escape.

Esther screamed in frustration. Picking up the pot, she threw it to the floor. It smashed into pieces.

"Just leave me alone."

Only desperate people contacted spiritualists. Her parents told her it wasn't a real religion, that it preyed on the vulnerable and profited from their grief. According to one website, spiritualists believed they could communicate with the dead, some using a spirit guide. They were able to pass messages to the living, and in some cases helped both parties find peace. Esther couldn't imagine Rufus ever being willing to find peace.

Gwendoline Sharp billed herself as a Spirit Medium. Her website explained she would be able to talk to the spirit in question, to find out why they couldn't leave the human plane. She'd then help them move on. Esther sent an email requesting a sitting.

*****

Alexander had told her she had a sweet telephone voice. Esther smiled. She hadn't noticed it until she reread the email. His irregular communication skills could be put to one side for the moment. She agreed to meet him for a meal the following week.

"It was a good week. The rain kept off and it was great to take the car out."

Esther tried to keep smiling, attempting to sound light.

"You didn't mention you were going away."

"I've been busy, and we had no plans so it didn't cross my mind."

Insignificant.

She forced a laugh, making a joke.

"How dare you."

Alexander laughed and looked at her.

"I couldn't forget."

He's lying.

"I'll have to take you out in my car. It's a convertible, a roadster in red. It's great fun to drive."

He could have asked her to go away with him.

It would have been a romantic thing to do. It hadn't even occurred to him. Her mood dropped and a heaviness pulled through her body, fixing her to her chair. Silence encased her.

Alexander continued:

"When the weather's nice we can take a trip into the country." He was smiling at her and he looked happy.

A balding middle-aged man in a cheap convertible.

Esther was embarrassed at the idea of being seen driving around town in a sports car.

What a cliché.

She'd always thought it the domain of sad men who have nothing better to do than make themselves look good by buying a showy car. The idea was awful. Cutting into her pizza, she kept her eyes down to avoid him.

You'd be an accessory to sadness.

"Have a picnic, maybe even the seaside? Whatever takes your fancy."

He pushed a large piece of pizza into his mouth.

Esther put her knife and fork down. She couldn't eat.

"Anything the matter?" She looked up at him and he was observing her with a slight frown. She shook her head.

"She's gone again. Earth to Esther, earth to Esther, is anyone there?" Esther couldn't help but laugh.

"Sorry Alexander. I'm just tired, thank you."

"Eat up, your pizza will go cold." Esther picked up her knife and fork again.

"You have the most beautiful dark eyes." Alexander was gesturing with his knife. "Intelligent and mysterious."

He continued eating. Esther was overwhelmed. She wanted to tell him how kind he was, and patient, and that she realised she was being an idiot, and that it wasn't her fault. This wasn't how she really was. Her friends thought her funny and kind and thoughtful, and her family loved her.

"Thank you," was all she could say.

You belong to me.

*****

Alexander soon followed up with an offer to take her out in the car. Communicating with him via email gave her time to consider and reconsider her replies. She could keep Rufus away from the keyboard and make an attempt at being herself.

HELLO

Hello Esther – I have a bit of a cold. But one struggles on …

I did the 1st draft of a speech with power point yesterday, and this morning did a Q&A briefing. Waiting to hear back – but the line manager was kind and said it was looking good last evening. I expect lots of changes though – it is the nature of the process. Had a pre-brief with Minister yesterday on something else (Government, Top Secret, would have to kill you, etc...), and just been an observer in the meeting now. Tried not to cough and splutter too much. Failed.

Anyway, enough about all that. I have day tickets for a folk music festival this Saturday. A friend was supposed to attend, yet he is now otherwise engaged (???). I hoped you'd fill his shoes, not literally you understand. It's a good opportunity to take you out in the car. Let me know if you're free and interested.

How was the shoot? Keep on being you. Onwards.

Alexander

RE: HELLO

Hey Alexander,

Glad to hear from you, and that you're being productive and busy. Hope the cold isn't keeping you from too many meetings.

Thank you. The shoot went well. Only a little tight for time, which made it rushed towards the end. I think there will be enough for an interesting film. I'll start cutting next week.

I'd love to come along on Saturday. I'm not an expert on folk music, but I'm sure there's something for everybody.

In the spirit of cultural exchange I've attached, for your reading pleasure, one of my favourite stories. It's sad but beautiful. The language is so evocative and visual. I feel as if I can hear the rain and feel the breeze from the open window. If you don't enjoy it I will say no more on the topic. There's a lovely night-time cycling scene, which you may appreciate. To go with it I've attached some photographs of male cyclists from the 1920s. I think you'll appreciate the style of cycle and dress.

Please let me know the arrangement for Saturday. I'll look forward to a trip to the country.

Best,

Esther

RE: RE: HELLO

… nearly there. Director has given it the OK, subject to me adding a reference to the 'Right to Buy' clause in the Localism Bill. What is that, you may ask? If I told you – I would have to bore you. Deadline noon. Thank you for the story and photographs. I'll pick you up at 10.30.

AWP

*****

As she followed Gwendoline around her house, Esther saw her things as if they were new. She watched Gwen slide her hand across her duvet cover and remembered buying it with Rufus. It was their first item after moving in together. The large photographic print above the bed was one of Rufus's. It was a photograph he'd taken on a day out.

A series of images flashed through her mind as she recreated the outing. She was smiling in the picture, but it had been a terrible day. They couldn't find anywhere to eat and he'd blamed her for not making a reservation. They ended up having chips on the beach and he'd thrown them at her one at a time, forcing her to understand he didn't eat fish and chips on the beach.

Esther hadn't expected to like Gwen, but she did.

Watching her calm touch soothed Esther. It was as if she could touch her past and banish the misery.

"Thank you for sharing your home, Esther. I sense a lot of pain, but love too." She smiled at Esther.

It was so genuine, any cynicism Esther retained was dissolved.

"Possessions are important. They hold shared memories and bind us together. They keep us in the physical world."

Gwen had explained there were various ways of contacting spirits, but she heard the spirit and passed on messages. Esther had told her she had seen Rufus a number of times, although she had no way of controlling him. Gwen reassured her that was her job.

Esther gave Rufus's favourite camera to Gwen, as she said she needed an object to connect her to his spirit. They sat at the kitchen table opposite one another.

"This might be difficult. The spirits can be unpredictable, especially one as troubled as Rufus. Are you ready, Esther?"

Esther nodded. Gwen placed her hands on the camera and closed her eyes.

"Rufus, are you there? Come and join us." She paused.

Esther watched her, equally bemused and terrified. Gwen looked like a sleeping child with her eyes closed.

"Don't be afraid. I can help you." Again Gwen paused.

They sat in silence.

"He's here. I can sense him." Gwen kept her eyes closed. Esther could see nothing.

"Rufus, welcome. Is there anything you need my help with?" Gwen held her gentle smile in place, her voice soothing.

Esther saw Rufus leaning against the doorframe.

"Tell Esther how much I love her. That it's hard to let go." Esther couldn't believe his contrite words.

"Did you hear that, Esther?" Gwen opened her eyes and looked with loving care into Esther's eyes.

"Yes, but I don't believe him." Gwen's smile persisted and she held out her hand to Rufus. He walked over to the table and knelt down.

"It's hard to let go of everything and go into another life. He needs help. He needs to know you love him."

Esther didn't know what to do. She didn't love him. And she hadn't loved him when he died. But as he knelt at the table he seemed changed. Humble and quiet.

"Esther, give him the confidence to move on."

To get rid of him it was worth telling the lie. She looked down at his face. Lying wasn't her forte, but he'd been a good teacher. She tried to make her voice as loving and gentle as Gwen's.

"I love you Rufus, but you need to go now."

"That's good, Esther. Rufus, I'll help you now. Look for the light and walk towards it, don't be afraid."

He stood up, smiling at them both, and to Esther's utter astonishment, stepped towards the living room and was gone. Gwen, still smiling, closed her eyes, put her hands together and prayed. As Gwen's voice floated over her, Esther closed her eyes too and, unbidden, gave a heartfelt plea that it was over.

That night, Esther looked at her arm and the bruise had gone. It was incredible; Esther wished she'd done it sooner. She instinctively looked under the bed or in the wardrobe for him, but knew that was silly. It seemed he was gone, and for the second time in her life she spontaneously prayed in pure gratitude.

*****

Since Gwen's visit, Esther had slept well and Rufus hadn't troubled her at all. On Saturday morning Alexander picked her up on time. The car was not what she expected at all. It was vintage and cute. The headlamps looked like eager eyes, and it promised to zoom them along country roads to their destination. It was not the ostentatious Porsche of her imagination.

Alexander thanked her for her story, but said nothing else about it. It didn't surprise her. When she reread her email she was mortified at how pretentious she sounded – 'evocative and visual'. Arrgh. Then she'd never been a fan of folk music, too much fiddle-dee-dee for her taste, and she hadn't mentioned that to Alexander. She was still a bit annoyed that she was his second choice for company, but she wanted to spend the entire day with him.

"The sun's hot and the festival's waiting." Alexander kissed her on the cheek and held the door open for her. The roof was down and he offered her a scarf to tie around her head.

"You should wear your sunglasses too. It can get a bit gritty." Esther wondered what the joy of travelling in an open top car could be if you were at the mercy of the elements. She retrieved her glasses from her bag and put them on.

"You look very sophisticated, like a 1950s film star." Alexander kissed her cheek again. Esther blushed.

"Alexander, I've bought you a small gift. It was stupid to think you'd like that miserable story I sent you. Who wants to feel sad by choice."

She tried to laugh but couldn't hold her head

up. She was glad her sunglasses hid her eyes, even if they couldn't hide her red cheeks. "So I got you this." She held out a book, *The Ascent of Rum Doodle*. "It's funny in a similar way to *Three Men in a Boat*, which is one of my favourites – it makes me laugh out loud – but I thought you'd probably read that." Alexander took the book and read the back.

"Esther, this is very kind and thoughtful. I'm sure I'll find it jolly amusing. I'm just sorry I don't have anything for you." Esther shook her head.

"It's okay. I wouldn't have expected anything."

Esther was still embarrassed by the car, especially when they stopped at lights and other motorists peered at them from the insides of their cars and cyclists sat alongside them. She felt she was being judged as vulgar. But once they had got out into the country lanes, she began to enjoy herself. The speed was fun. Being low to the ground and watching the trees zip past exhilarated her.

"It's great, isn't it?" Alexander shouted above the sound of the engine.

"Apart from the wind." She shouted loud to make herself heard, and then laughed because shouting was something bad but this was good.

"A drink, I think." Alexander led her by the hand through the crowd, looking back to make sure she was following as they walked towards the beer tent. It was the first time they'd held hands and she was beaming. Groups of middle-aged men with greying beards mingled with young men sporting fashionable full beards. Music filtered through the air and the Cajun violin lifted her mood even further. Girls with long floral dresses and others with slim legs leading down to cowboy boots or strappy sandals moved around each other, dancing to the music. She felt buoyant and light.

After getting their drinks, they made their way to a grassy bank a generous distance from the stage, but near enough to enjoy the music. For the first time she was able to chat with ease. She told him about her family. Her dad was a plumber and her mum stayed at home to look after them. Her dad was insistent they all had professions that would give them a steady income and a stable life. Her eldest sister had become a GP, her middle sister a dentist, and her little brother a lawyer. Her parents were so proud of them.

Esther had gone against her dad's stipulations and attended art college. It had caused the entire family a lot of upset. Her father was worried she'd struggle with financial insecurity and told her she was wasting her time. They'd stopped speaking for a few years, but her eldest sister had convinced him that Esther had to do what she felt was right. Her sisters loved her but she knew they didn't understand her need to be creative, and they tolerated her choices rather than supported her. Esther didn't tell Alexander that one of the reasons she had endured the creative industry for so long was because she couldn't bear to admit to her family that they'd been right. Or that she hadn't told them how hard she found her work, or that Rufus's being a successful photographer had been a way to prove to them that they were wrong. Art was a solid career. When they'd finally expressed pride in the way her life had worked out, she knew she couldn't ever tell them how miserable she was or what a mess she'd made of everything.

Alexander told her he only had an elder brother, but they were strictly forbidden to argue. It upset their parents too much and in consequence they hadn't had a cross word in over thirty years.

"I love this band. They're the best folk act the UK has to offer. Let's get nearer." Alexander stood up and offered Esther his hand and helped her get to her feet. Once again, he led her through the crowd. As they got nearer to the stage the density of people increased until Alexander was unable to hold onto her hand and they were forced apart.

"Stay here. This is near enough." He shouted to her across half a dozen bearded faces. Esther watched the band on tiptoe, trying to see all the members dotted about the stage. She looked around to find Alexander. At first she couldn't see him and then she noticed he was holding hands with a young woman. Esther was astounded – she couldn't believe what he was doing, she felt sick and dizzy. Her strength gone, Esther forced her way to Alexander.

"What are you doing," she shouted, "with that girl?" Alexander was stunned. He looked around for the girl.

"What? Her?" He pointed to a girl carrying a large bag of leaflets.

"I saw you, I saw you holding hands behind my back with that girl."

"She was just giving out leaflets. Our hands touched for a moment. Not on purpose, I might add." He tried to shrug it off, holding up the colourful leaflet.

"No, I saw you were holding hands. I'm not an idiot."

Rufus laughed, his laugh alternated from one ear to the other as if he were spinning around her. The sound was dizzying. He'd tricked her. He hadn't gone anywhere. The spiritualist had been a failure. This moment was a memory from Rufus. Rufus had been holding hands with a girl at a concert they'd gone to for her birthday. It had only been a few months before their wedding. She had known this was the moment she should have ended the relationship, but no one had believed her. They'd said she'd been seeing things, that he wouldn't do such a thing, so she'd left it, feeling unsure of her own judgement. Now Rufus had let her relax long enough to see what a relationship with Alexander could be like and allowed her to think it was going to be okay. Once again, the bruise on her arm ached.

"I can't believe this, Esther. I think we should go home." Alexander was stern, his usual jovial manner gone. Esther panicked; she wanted to take it all back and make it okay again.

"Please, please, please, Alexander, it was a mistake. I thought, I don't know, it was a mistake. Please can't we stay and just enjoy the day. We were having a lovely time. We were having a lovely time." She grabbed him around the neck and tried to kiss him. Alexander removed her arms and placed them at her side. She sobbed. Members of the crowd jostled past her, pushing her in various directions.

"I'm sorry, I'm sorry, I'm sorry." Esther covered her face, she didn't want him to see her anymore. She was drained.

Alexander grabbed hold of her wrist and pulled her back through the crowd. As soon as they were at a safe distance he hugged her.

"You have the saddest face when you cry. I can't bear it." Holding her until she stopped crying, he continued. "How about we take a slow drive home? We'll find somewhere to stop and eat." Esther nodded and wiped the tears from her cheeks with the cuff of her sleeve.

She could feel him lying behind her. His cigarette smoke drifted into the air, curling around her body. He was laughing in between sucking on his cigarette.

Vicars and spiritualists. Pitiful.

Everything ached and she was desperate to sleep and shut him out of her consciousness. The more she tried to escape him the more he persisted, breathing hatred into her ear.

Was that the best you could do?

Actually, it had been. It was hopeless and there was no one to help her. He was destroying her mind and spirit. She'd been an idiot to think she'd get away from him.

*****

"And he was okay after that?" Daisy held a Danish swirl mid-air, ready to bite.

"Yes, he was really kind. Let me forget all about it and even paid for dinner."

Daisy spoke despite the bun lodged in her cheek. "He's a keeper. How many men do you know would put up with that kind of shit?" Esther shrugged. "Let's face it, everything you've told me about the way you've been acting is crazy. Right off the bunny boiling scale, and you look terrible."

She swallowed her mouthful and put the bun down.

"Seriously Est, you've got to get it together, and not just for him, or you're gonna send yourself mad."

"I know but …"

"But what? That means more crazy talk." Daisy raised a warning eyebrow.

"But he doesn't answer his phone, he didn't tell me he was going away and …"

"And nothing. You've only been seeing him a couple of months. He doesn't owe you anything."

"But he's acting just like Rufus. The absences and delays. I've been down this road before, Daze. It's exactly the same."

"Are you kidding me? Dufus was the biggest loser on earth."

Esther leant in close to Daisy. She whispered, "He's here, Daisy."

"Who? Who do you mean?"

"Rufus. I hear him and see him. He won't leave me alone."

Daisy put her coffee down and stared at Esther. "No, he's not. It just feels like it. He put you through hell and I'm not surprised you're still feeling it."

"Daze, it's more than that. He's in my head, controlling me."

"Esther. He's not. The only person controlling you is you. I think you need to tell Alex about Rufus."

"He'll run a mile, no man wants that kind of baggage."

"And no man wants a sulking, erratic, emotional woman weeping at him either. Sort it out, or if you're not ready, move on."

He'd said seven-thirty at The Sparrow. She'd been early so she'd already been waiting nearly forty-five minutes. His email was clear; she'd checked it over and again, she was definitely in the right place at the right time. He'd sent no message to explain his delay, if it was a delay.

He's not coming.

Every time the pub door opened, her head automatically turned to see who came in. Relief was followed by frustration. She tried to read, but the words jumped in front of her defying her understanding. She checked her phone again. There was still no message. She promised herself she'd wait another five minutes maximum, then after that another five until it became twenty. He'd given up on her. Her relief surprised her. She could put an end to all the worry and go back to her single life. Hope had been a burden. But she had so wanted this to work. Frantic and lost, she waited.

"Esther, you're still here. Thank heavens." Alexander approached the table, dumped his things and bent down to kiss her.

Wait for the excuses.

Esther dodged him. In a second her joy at seeing him turned to hurt.

"I'm sorry I'm late. I've lost my mobile and I've been at a conference in Birmingham all day." He did sound sorry.

There's always a way.

"Why didn't you email, or ring the pub?" Esther asked.

Alexander sighed.

"I didn't have your contact details and I don't have a laptop. I'm getting a drink. Do you want one?" Esther shook her head. Alexander went off to the bar.

Do you believe that?

Esther didn't, but there was no reason why she shouldn't. It was incredible he didn't have any way of getting in contact with her. Alexander returned and placed his drink on the table.

"Is this seat taken? My name's Alexander." He held out his hand. Esther wouldn't smile, but nodded.

"Go ahead, sit down." She watched as he pulled the seat out and sat down. She loved the way he moved, his limbs loose and quick.

"I've had a hell of a day. It's the new post, I have to go all over for the first few months until it settles down." He gulped his beer. "Good pint." He inspected his glass.

"I thought you'd forgotten." Esther mumbled half into her glass.

"Not at all. Why would you think that?" Esther shrugged.

"I suppose." She stopped.

"Suppose what? Come on, you can't start and then just stop."

"It's boring."

"I want to know."

So she told him about her marriage to Rufus. About how he'd betrayed her, insulted and controlled her, and physically hurt her. This was too much misery for Alexander. He was furious and wanted to hurt Rufus and make it okay for her. He found it difficult to understand why she'd stayed with Rufus. Esther couldn't explain that he'd been fascinating and popular. He'd been wry and clever and everybody admired him because he had all the attributes anyone could ever want: talent, unconventionality, and the correct politics. He was charming, said all the right things, and dressed the right way. None of his friends had known what a bully he really was. They knew he was erratic, but it had been attributed to an artistic temperament, which made him even more attractive. Esther confessed, she was one of those people who made that excuse for him too.

"I can't say I understand any of it, Esther. I've had a very boring life, but I do know that you can't let the past haunt you. It can't hurt you now." Alexander smiled at her.

*****

Bucket cunt.

She wanted to sleep with Alexander; it would make their relationship more secure, but she was scared. She feared a repeat of the cake-hole kiss. Even being in someone else's bedroom was alien and she wasn't sure what she should do. Sitting on the bed, she waited for him to take the lead. It wasn't supposed to be like this. They should have been snogging and ripping each other's clothes off as soon as they got into the house. Alexander took his coat off and hung it on a stand in the corner.

"Don't you want to take your coat off?" He sat next to her and unlaced his boots. Esther stood up and started unfastening her coat buttons.

Loose and sloppy.

She wanted to cry. They'd got this far and this was what she had wanted. He'd see her body and pubic hair and she'd see his dick. Dick – it was a horrible word, it was the word Rufus always used. It made her feel ashamed. She blinked to dismiss her tears.

Overused, abused.

The room was cold but Alexander opened the window.

"I like fresh air. Don't worry, we'll soon snuggle up and get warm." Esther shivered from the breeze and hugged herself, but the idea of snuggling made her smile.

"Snuggling. Is that what you call it?" she asked him. He laughed aloud.

Lying awake she stared around the semi-dark room. Orange light from a street lamp directly outside the window gave the room an unreal glow. It was stark and contained a bed, set of drawers and a hat stand. Apart from the coats, two suits and half a dozen shirts hung from it. On a shelf above the set of drawers was a large, vintage style DAB radio. Arranged on the drawers were two watches and some cufflinks. A row of boots lined up under the windows. She needed to go to the toilet, but was afraid to move. Alexander slept next to her on his back. His mouth was wide open and he snored loudly at regular intervals. Esther watched him for a moment, trying to work out if he'd wake up if she moved. He might be angry if she woke him. With care, she peeled back the cover and swung her legs over the edge of the bed. The room was freezing. She crept towards her clothes and put on her jumper and left the room.

Black make-up was smeared across her face and her hair was awry. She looked awful. There was a brush at the side of the sink so she picked it up intending to arrange her hair, but wound around its handle was a hair band.

He's seeing someone else.

Esther was shocked. Alexander's flatmate didn't have a girlfriend, and this was the first time she'd been to his new house. It was possible Alexander was seeing someone else. They only saw each other twice a week. It would be easy for him to have other relationships. When she'd found a hairband in Rufus's bathroom, she'd forced herself to ask him what it meant. He'd protested that it was his and he used it to keep his hair from his face when washing. He'd even demonstrated by pulling his short fringe into bunch and attempting to put the band around it. It didn't hold. It was more evidence she could have used to justify leaving, but still she'd made excuses.

Look at his phone.

Rufus was standing with his head resting on her

shoulder, looking at her in the mirror, as if he too had been asleep and she'd just woken him.

What she was doing was a betrayal of trust. If she couldn't believe what he told her it made their relationship a lie. She crept back to the bedroom.

It's the only way to be sure.

Gently she lifted the flap up on his bag, lowered her hand in and retrieved his phone. Alexander was still snoring. She took the phone to the landing, just in case he woke up. The list of messages appeared, she scrolled down: Mum, Monty, Doug, and then she saw Ella. She clicked on the text.

Will we see you for curry this weekend? Pocałunki.

She had no idea who Ella was. 'We' suggested someone else too. Even if this woman wasn't a love interest, he'd never mentioned her.

Now you can't ask.

Esther was crushed. Alexander told her nothing.

You're so fucking gullible.

This was unacceptable. She was unacceptable. She

wouldn't let herself become this person, someone like Rufus. She wouldn't use such methods to make herself feel better. Being alone or being left with Rufus was preferable to making someone else's life a misery. Everything else she'd tried had failed. Instead, she had to do something to change her life. She decided she wouldn't see Alexander again, even if it hurt her. It was her only option.

Her life was divided between work and home. She worked long hours and made sure she was ahead, researching potential new projects and writing extra proposals to show she had ingenuity and ideas. She'd been told that she was thorough in her work, but was too shy, not speaking up to defend her suggestions. She wanted it to change.

Esther also cleaned. The house was full of rubbish. Every cupboard spewed paper, and chaotic knick-knacks were forced into nooks, and drawers spilled over and wouldn't shut with the amount of things trapped behind them. Her grief at giving up Alexander turned into action. She started with the paperwork. There were three cupboards with a surfeit of papers that had been squeezed in between one another, growing until they were so tight together Esther couldn't get her fingers between them. She chose a Saturday night and pulled them all onto the floor, turned on the television, poured a glass of wine and started to sort. Esther hadn't done anything to the house since Rufus had disappeared and she knew she'd find old documents belonging to him. Preparing herself, she made various piles including one that would be for his things. Mostly the papers were old bills and statements, some were leaflets and tickets for exhibitions she'd been to, even some prospectuses for courses she'd considered taking.

She came across a thick letter. Straight away she knew it wasn't hers. The handwriting was small, the letters regular and consistent. She took the letter from its envelope and began to read. It was from Rufus's ex-partner and was a summary of their relationship. Pages long, there were various headings detailing all the problems they'd encountered, mainly problems with him: depression, affairs, family, abuse, Esther, and separation. It was dated only two months before their wedding. The tone was more like an academic proposal than that of the jilted girlfriend, and implied they were more than just lovers but partners in a way that Esther and Rufus had never been. But it was desperate too. The final paragraph stunned her.

This relationship you have chosen with Esther

is an expression of all that I have discussed through-out the letter. I feel sure when you have had time to reconsider, you will see our twelve years together are worth more than this woman can offer you. I under-stand she is younger than me, attractive and part of your new set of London friends, but these things are ephemeral, true love remains. I have seen you dis-tracted by others and I have no doubt she will not be the last. When you've suffered, I've been there for you and no one understands your past or your depression in the same way as I do. I have faith that we will be together again and I will be here for you when you are ready to return.

Yours always,
Melanie

This poor woman had thrown twelve years of her life away on Rufus. Esther felt sorry for her. At least she'd only wasted three. The saddest thing about it was the formal tone, as if reason could persuade him to love her, could persuade him to be some other man than he really was. It was like asking a lion not to eat a wounded zebra. She had looked after him for years, tolerating his erratic, volatile behaviour, allowing him to see other women and providing him with a home. He was a spoilt child. Esther realised his behaviour had nothing to do with her. It wasn't about her at all. She'd just been unfortunate enough to marry him. Unfortunate, gullible and vulnerable. He'd been right about her and had helped her to stay that way. But she couldn't let him get away with it anymore or continue to dictate the choices she made. She would fight him.

Meeting his friends was important to Alexander. Blocking out Rufus, Esther had to prove she could make it work with Alexander. Since she'd found the letter, their relationship had been calmer, more relaxed, and she'd seen nothing from Rufus. But he was sure to re-emerge with one of his tricks.

Alexander had known Ella and Steve for years. They'd all lived together before Ella and Steve became a couple. Hearing about Ella made Esther worried. Alexander talked about her in such an intimate way, it made her feel excluded. He'd said when she first arrived in London from Poland her mother had come with her and made Alexander and Steve promise they'd look after her. The stories Alexander told Esther to endear Ella to her had made her wary. This woman had been the sole focus of two men for years; Esther wasn't sure Ella would accept another woman into their group.

Esther had already drunk two glasses of wine before Ella and Steve arrived. She didn't want to be the silent group member, as well as an outsider. As they made their way across the restaurant, Alexander stepped forward and greeted them. He shook Steve's hand, but grabbed Ella. They held onto each other for a long time.

"Angel, is good to see you." Ella stroked Alexander's face. "You have lost weight – is not for the better." She kissed him on the lips and then held onto his hands. She kept holding onto his hand, as Alexander introduced her to Esther.

"You have beautiful long hair," Ella commented. "But mine is short, cut from being long because these two prefer it." Ella nodded and smiled and continued. "All that long hair was too much, it's more stylish short."

Esther was aghast at everything that had taken place in the last minute, but still it went on.

"This style," Ella gestured to her 20s style bobbed hair, "is Alexander's favourite style."

Esther's silence was absolute. Her voice had been taken from her and dropped into the bottom of the ocean. They sat down at the table and the others chatted. They talked about work, Alexander's new bike, of which Ella didn't approve as she felt sure he'd be killed, and what they'd been doing since they'd last met.

"But we're being rude. We can catch up later, you're here to meet Esther." Alexander held her hand and kissed it. "Esther does some really interesting things in her work. She's very creative. Unlike me." Esther was grateful for his intervention.

"Yes, it's very varied and I get a chance to explore lots of different areas of art." Esther relaxed again, knowing Alexander was still thinking about her.

"It's an arts magazine, isn't it?" Steve looked like he had genuine interest.

"Yes, but I work on the website."

"How does it work?" he asked.

"The magazine editor decides which features she wants and then I adapt and upload them on the website. Sometimes it might be putting up the entire transcript of an interview that there wasn't room for in the magazine. But, most interesting for me, I get to explore trends in the art world more fully or feature lesser-known artists. That kind of thing." Esther was pleased with herself. She grinned, happy that she had talked about her work with such confidence.

"But is just the internet, not the real magazine," Ella said.

"Ella, don't be a pain," Steve warned her.

"I have more flexibility and control. There are only two of us working on the website, so as long as I can justify it, I can do lots of good stuff. At the moment I'm working on the theme of Wanderlust on the back of the Joseph Cornell exhibition, but I'm bringing in works of literature and ideas around psychogeography. When it's done it's going to be really interesting."

"But still on the web, not a real magazine." Ella shrugged.

"Ella," Steve warned again.

"Is true." She shrugged again.

"I think it sounds wonderful and I'll be very interested to read it." Alexander kissed her on the cheek.

"You often say, 'Art isn't your thing,'" Ella said. Alexander ignored her.

"Well now, what shall we eat? I'm famished." He picked the menu up and began to read. They all stared at their menus.

"What will you have, Esther? You're too thin, order plenty," Ella encouraged.

"I'll have a Vesuvius with extra artichoke please." Esther handed her menu back to the waiter.

"That's my favourite too, I love artichoke. We are same."

Esther was horrified at the idea. After all the orders had been taken, the conversation resumed, but this time for her benefit. Ella explained how her 'angel' Alexi had been there when she'd got together with Steve and when they got married. They spent all their birthdays together and she would die of loneliness if it were any other way. Alexander was her second husband, she held his hand across the table as she said it. Esther stared at Ella and then at Alexander. They seemed to betray no thought that it might be inappropriate. The food arrived and broke up their intimacy. Ella turned to her.

"Are you happy with your family?" Esther wanted to laugh at her phrasing.

"My parents are happy enough, they bicker a lot." Esther smiled, imagining her parents' brisk exchange of predictable unpleasantries.

"Mine never argue. They are perfect. They give me everything I need." Ella grinned, showing her canines.

"Alexander's parents are lovely people. And his brother's so handsome."

"I haven't met them," Esther conceded.

"I didn't think so." Ella bared her teeth again.

This was too much. She had tried but failed to be part of the group, but she'd just ended up boring them about art and it clearly wasn't 'their thing'. She was an outsider. Esther got up from the table, and as gracefully as possible, walked away.

Esther stood in the toilet cubicle, crying. Ella was so hurtful and Alexander appeared to have no idea. She felt abandoned. It had been ten minutes and she knew that if she didn't want Alexander to find out she'd been crying she'd have to return soon. Esther heard the toilet door open.

"Esther come back. We'll have dessert. Don't stay here, be good," Ella shouted through the cubicle door.

She pities you.

His voice was smug. Her arm ached. Rufus was back. Esther was determined she wouldn't let him control her. She swallowed back her tears and flushed the toilet.

"You go on. I'll be there in a minute."

"Okay, but hurry." Esther waited until she heard the toilet door close and then she emerged from the cubicle. Her face was tear stained, her eyes sore and red. It would be difficult to pretend she was having a good time.

They'll never accept you.

"I'm sorry Alexander, I'm not feeling very well. Do you mind if we go?" He scrutinised her face.

"Sorry to hear it. You don't look very well." He turned to Steve.

"Sorry Steve, but I'll see you next week for a curry." Steve stood up as well.

"No problem, take her home and look after her." They shook hands. Esther was getting her coat on as Ella and her Alexi hugged.

"You, my angel, see you soon." Ella stroked his

face again. Esther turned away.

Alexander took her hand as they walked along the road heading for the station.

"Sorry you're not well Esther, it would have been nice to go for a drink afterwards."

Esther said nothing. Her sadness was creeping its way up out of her stomach and into her throat. Tears blurred her vision. It was incredible that he had no idea how awful the evening had been for her and how hurt she had been by both him and Ella.

"Sorry," she mumbled. Alexander looked at her and stopped walking.

"What's wrong, you're not crying again are you?"

He doesn't want you.

"Again. You say it as if I don't have a reason." Esther couldn't hold her tears back.

"There's no need to cry just because you're feeling unwell."

You're damaged goods.

Esther couldn't cope any longer. She shouted. "Shut up, shut up! When will I ever be special to anyone?" Her breath came short and erratic through her sobs.

Sloppy seconds.

"Why don't you want to love me? Why is it always so hard?"

Alexander just stood staring at her. "You can't even manage one evening without getting upset. This was supposed to be a pleasant meal with friends. What is wrong with you?"

You're all wrong.

"What's wrong with me?" Esther screamed. "Me? Your friend's a bitch, she's mean and you didn't even notice, and the way you two touch each other is sick and twisted. You'd rather be part of her harem than have me. You don't care about me." Esther was hysterical.

"You don't think I care? I've been patient because I like you, I think you're worth the effort, don't you?" Alexander was shouting too.

You don't deserve to live.

"Worth the effort!" Her voice was now a screech of incredulity. "Don't bother if I'm that much trouble, Alexander."

"You're not the only one that's scared. It is scary to trust someone and change your life. But I've had enough." Alexander turned to leave. Rufus was laughing.

"You can't leave. Don't leave." She followed behind him, grabbing onto his sleeve as he walked. He stopped and removed her hand.

"Go home, Esther."

Crazy bitch.

Esther didn't know what to do, she was frantic.

He's leaving you.

Rufus laughed.

She slapped Alexander across the face. Rufus guffawed. Alexander was stunned for a moment, then continued walking away. Esther sobbed, crouching down on the ground as she watched him turn the corner into the next street.

Now you're mine.

Esther lay in the bath, her mouth level with the surface of the water. Rufus was right. Alexander didn't want her. Everything that Rufus had said was right. No one else would want her. He passed her a glass full of wine. She gulped at it until it was empty.

You're unlovable.

Rufus sat on the edge of the bath watching her and smiling. He gave her another glass and she drained it. She'd lied to her parents and couldn't admit how lonely she was. How miserable. Daisy was her only friend, but even she'd move on and forget all about Esther in time.

Only I want you.

Everything that was good had been ruined and Esther didn't know how to make it right. Alexander had been a chance to forget about her failure, but she couldn't make it work. She was incapable.

Only I love you.

Incapable of being amongst other people. Since childhood, it was as if she was observing them through a screen, and when she tried to speak they looked for the speaker but couldn't see or understand her. Her words never had the impact she expected and eventually she'd taken refuge behind flippant humour: that had made everyone more comfortable. She'd failed at work and was continually terrified of being discovered a fraud. Nothing she did was ever easy and she was tired of trying.

No need to keep trying.

She guzzled another glass of wine. The alcohol and heat made her body heavy and leaden in the water. She had no more tears.

Come with me.

Esther relaxed and slipped under the water. Rufus held his hand on her head. Through the water, she could see him smiling down at her, his features distorted into grotesque shapes. Surrendering herself, she allowed him to keep her submerged and she breathed. Water filled her nose and mouth. Esther let go, trusting Rufus would make everything okay. He kept pushing her down. Her eyes were open, staring up at him, and she was silent as the water entered her airways. Distorted sounds surrounded her, carried through the water, compounding together words formed from Rufus's lips. Indistinct, they roused memories and she heard Alexander telling her he was scared and saying she was worth the effort. Rufus had tricked her into surrender. Esther didn't want to go with Rufus. She wanted life. She wanted Alexander.

Esther thrashed as the water entered her lungs. She fought, dragging his arm from her head, struggling to be free. He pushed down harder. Through the blur, she could see Rufus's smile of contempt and his total concentration as he leant on her. But this time she attacked. Forcing her arms in all directions, she wrestled until his grip slipped and her head broke above the water. Rasping and spitting, half-choked and almost dead, Esther pulled herself from the water. She lay on the bathroom floor breathing hard, exhausted but determined to live.

*****

No one could help her. Esther now understood that. She had to end this for herself. She had to hold her own exorcism and she didn't need anyone else's help. She no longer even wanted it.

Everything that had belonged to Rufus, anything he'd bought her and all the wedding gifts they'd been given, she built into a funeral pyre in the back garden. She'd chosen an ancient pagan ritual, in which fire was deemed to be the transformative power of the universe. He'd burned her, and now she'd burn him. His shoes jutted out from amongst tangled clothes.

Camera and computer equipment formed a techno-logical peak resting on an upturned easy chair, while hundreds of old CDs slid down the side.

Esther was ready to begin.

"All things are an interchange for fire, and fire for all things, just like goods for gold and gold for goods. I ask the universe to exchange his spirit for my life."

Her breath was visible before her, showing that her words had made it into the world. She threw Melanie's letters onto the bonfire, except for one. The match fizzed into life and she held it against Melanie's final letter. Orange flame crept across the paper leaving black specks of ash in the air. When the flames were strong enough she threw it onto the pile of things. For a moment she watched the fire burn and then she picked up the framed photograph from the bedroom. Holding it before her she shouted:

"For every time you shouted, sulked, and bullied."

WorthlessPatheticNeedyDesperateUnlovable

Rufus spat his venom at Esther but she continued shouting louder.

"Your words can no longer hurt me."

She threw the picture onto the fire. The glass smashed and the photo curled at the heat. She picked up her wedding dress.

"All things are an interchange for fire, and fire for all things. I ask the universe to exchange his spirit for my life."

The flames engulfed it. Glass popped and china smashed as the heat of the fire increased. The laptop was bending, and rubber soles were melting. Rufus bit into her arm. She ignored him and the pain, determined on her ritual. She continued.

"I was beautiful and you were too ugly to see. Everything you said and did was ugly. I will no longer see you."

Rufus's bile-fuelled scream cut into the night air.

StupidWhoreInaneInadequateAbusedUsed

She shouted over him.

"All things are an interchange for fire, and fire for all things. I ask the universe to exchange his spirit for my life."

His anger was obvious from his contorted face, spit flying from his mouth. He writhed, moving around the pyre as if he were physically burning in the flames. She picked up the first gift he'd given her. It was a beautiful book of photographic portraits. Inside the cover was an inscription: *The beginning of your education, with love, Rufus.* She'd thought it insulting at the time but had said nothing.

"You were my education. But you taught me all the wrong things. Now I burn those lessons and will learn new ones. All things are an interchange for fire, and fire for all things. I ask the universe to exchange his spirit for my life."

The book burnt well. Everything must be destroyed. Rufus continued to thrash around the pyre, his figure gradually fusing with the flames. Finally, all the letters and cards they had exchanged. All their words of love.

"These words were lies. We both lied. Love is kind, generous and patient. I will have love in my life."

Esther dropped each piece of paper separately into the flames. The fire was ablaze. It was furious and hot; she had to take a step backwards to watch it burn. As the flames danced, Rufus was reduced to a flicker at the corner of her eye; a flicker that gradually slowed to a pulse and then disappeared. He had fought but she'd proved stronger. Esther stared as the flames reached high into the air. The smell of the damp autumn air blended with the smoke infused with rubber, paper, metal and fabric. She shouted:

"You can't hurt me. You are dead and gone."

*****

Esther was happy in her new life. She couldn't afford the mortgage on their old house and had bought a flat in a quieter neighbourhood. Rufus would have hated it. It wasn't Boho chic. It was stable, solid, and hers. Work had improved and she had grown in confidence, unafraid to suggest ideas. Overcoming her shyness, some colleagues became friends. She went out with them to the pub, to parties, to festivals. She was living.

The bruise took months to entirely disappear. The teeth marks that had scarred her skin healed first. Then the purple faded to a dirty yellow. Eventually even that was erased, just as completely as Rufus himself.

She had thought about Alexander a lot. She missed him, but it wasn't reasonable to think he would want to be with her. At least she owed him an explanation and apology.

21.32 TO BRISTOL TEMPLE MEADS

Dear Alexander,

I hope you're well and don't mind me getting in contact with you.

Mainly I want to apologise about the way I behaved during our relationship. You were nothing but understanding, patient and kind. I was totally unreasonable and am unreservedly sorry for any harm or upset I caused you.

I shared some of my past experiences that led me to act as I did, but as you said, you can't let the past haunt you. I've done everything I can to move on and conquer my demons.

Alexander, I'm mostly sorry that I wasn't able to trust and be with you. I liked you and still do, but I'll have to live with my regret.

Wishing you all the best and much love,

Esther Mitchell

The automatic reply appeared in Esther's inbox. She smiled. She knew he'd reply as soon as he could. If he wanted to.

WRITER BIOGRAPHY

© Bernard Zieja

Sarah Gray has been storytelling all her professional life. As a writer and filmmaker she loves to explore the darkly comic side of life.

Surface Tension is the first of a triptych of short-story collections, depicting the uncanny worlds of her imagination. Sarah lives in London.

Visit Sarah's website at: sarahgrayracontesse.com